Happy Trails

For Land's Sake

For Land's Sake

Charles Chupp

Chupp Publishing, Inc.
DeLeon, Texas

This is a work of fiction. Names, characters, places, and incidents are either the product of the author's imagination or are used fictitiously, and any resemblance to actual persons, living or dead, business establishments, events or locales is entirely coincidental.

FIRST EDITION

Copyright © 2001
By Charles Chupp

Chupp Publishing, Inc.

Manufactured in the United States of America
Printed by Sunbelt Media
Austin, Texas

ALL RIGHTS RESERVED.

ISBN 1-57168-955-9

For CIP information,
please access:
www.loc.gov

acknowledgments

First off, I'm much obliged to Kent and Celia Boswell, Georgia Ann Fields, and Fred Turner. I don't wish to give an edge to any one 'em so you'll note that they're listed in alphabetical order. How they aided and abetted me is of scant interest to you readers—but they know, and so do I.

The colorful right of way agents I've known over the years are too numerous to catalog, and some of them might offer to dot my eye for their inclusion, so they shall remain nameless.

Most of all, I'm indebted to my bride of fifty years. Her toleration of me has earned her Sainthood, and she ain't through yet. Margaret has stuck with me through thick and thin, and sometimes it would have made more sense to run away from home.

But, she's still here, and all is right with the world.

chapter 1

Ben saw the ribbon of snake a hundred yards ahead, and instinctively eased his foot from the accelerator onto the brake. The new sun was making its way over the horizon and the reflected broadside segments of the snake glistened like neon as it worked a zig zag route toward the shallow bar ditch and meager cover of broom weed and scrub mesquite. That snake had most likely spent the cool of the early spring night on the warm road surface.

The Ford Tempo stopped within ten feet of the crossing and Ben watched as the rattler left the oil soaked lease road. It was at least a five footer and sported a sizable length of beads in its rattle. It took discipline not to rev up and flatten a rattlesnake when he got the chance, but Ben sat and waited just in case the mate might be tagging along. Not that he was going to run over it if there was a second one, he had broken the habit of flattening rattlesnakes, a good while back.

Back in the spring of '79 he'd been traveling a similar lease road down in Crain County when he got the opportunity to snuff a rattler. He'd put his left front tire across that one's middle, and was pleased and satisfied to hear the succession of thumps as the snake collided with the underside of his vehicle. "One less sidewinder!" he'd smiled with satisfaction.

Unfortunately, he only ran halfway over that snake. It tangled up in the undercarriage and rode forty miles to the Ramada Inn in Vast Plain. When Ben alit at his room, that snake slithered out and struck his roughout boot with the suddenness and force of a lightning bolt. Luckily, the fangs had broken off due to the collision or the wild ride and the stubs did not pierce the leather. He dispatched that snake with a jack handle, hurried into his room and changed into dry underwear. Since then, he'd curbed any inclination to run over rattlesnakes. Just the recall would raise the hair on the back of his neck.

Satisfied that he'd see no parade, he resumed his interrupted journey to the Kelly ranch. The radio was tuned to KRIG in Midway and Coy Works was spinning Country Classics for his audience in the great Permian Basin. Ben sang "City Lights", along with Ray Price. He knew the lyrics as well as Ray, and most of the words to most of the recorded country and western songs of the past thirty years. His singing voice might not be the equal of the professionals, but his repertoire was second to none. He'd honed his word recall in thirty-five years of on the job travel, averaging better than a hundred thousand miles a year. He'd worn out a Ford every year during that span, but he'd never worn out a radio, and since he traveled alone, his singing didn't abuse any ears except his own.

As Ben neared the house he clicked the radio off, and eased to a stop in the goathead sticker infested, unfenced, debris littered expanse, which served as a front yard. He shook his head at the mess and rolled the window glass halfway down, but he did not get out. He sat quietly with the motor still running and tried to see into the darkness beneath the front porch.

He'd not been to the Kelly place for a good while, but he remembered the big yellow dog that had put him on the hood of his car on that visit. He'd made the mistake of getting out, and was almost to the porch when that growling dog charged and almost overtook him before he could jump to the hood of his car. Biting dogs are standard equipment at most of the remote dwellings in West Texas, and Goose Kelly's sentry ranked in the top ten of the Permian Basin species. At least, that was Ben's belief.

On that occasion he had been to see Goose Kelly about a two-mile length of 69KV electric line right of way. The negotiations had spanned two months and Ben made a dozen trips to dicker with Goose Kelly. Ben was as patient as Job when negotiations were underway, and his patience had paid off. He hoped he hadn't used all his patience last time. Goose Kelly could be a trying man.

He could not recall the dog's name, but he whistled softly and called for him to come out. Nothing stirred, and Ben's hope that Goose might be away with his dog seemed to be a good bet. He'd already made up his mind to drive up to Carlsbad for breakfast and coffee, if the trip turned out to be a water haul. It was only a two-hour drive, and Ben hungered for some home made gravy and biscuits—served up by Brenda. Brenda was actually more interesting to Ben than the food, but the sixty-weight gravy was widely known and admired around south New Mexico and the adjoining west Texas area. So was Brenda.

Ben seldom made appointments with people like Goose Kelly. He believed blindsiding was the best way to gain the initial interview—with men like Goose.

Ben got out, leaving the door ajar just in case that dog was lurking under the house. He walked toward the three riser plank steps and called Mr. Kelly's name. A well service truck rattled by on the lease road but there was no sound of life in the house. Ben knocked on the rattletrap screen door and listened intently for a radio or television set. Nothing.

Joyfully, Ben leaped from the porch and was almost back to his car when he heard the protesting groan of the screen doorframe, as it scraped open.

"Who the hell's that banging on my door?" Goose was on the premises.

chapter II

Kent Fields downed two cups of coffee before Lilly set his scrambled eggs and crisp bacon on the snack bar. He picked up his fork and a triangle of toast, but his normal breakfast appetite had not come to the table with him. He had a lot on his mind since that meeting yesterday with his supervisor, Marv Freeman. Something bad was about to happen in the Sales and Customer Relations Department at Texas Lighting Company, or TLC, according to the acronym and logo.

Kent had tossed and worried the night away and what sleeping he'd done had not been the sort that refreshes. He was weary from the effort of trying to sleep, and was trying to decide whether he should involve Lilly in his problem and if so—how to go about it. The information Marv had imposed on him had cost him a night's sleep, and he couldn't get it off his mind.

"We need to talk Kent," Marv had begun as soon as Kent closed the door and found a chair.

"Let's do it," Kent said as he lit a smoke and slouched down in the padded chair. "That's the way I make my living," he laughed, but Marv did not even smile.

"Management has advised me that TLC is going to lean down. We've got to reduce our employee head count ten percent within the next ninety days. Our department has twenty employees—so that means I'm going to lose two—whether I like it or not. And of course, I don't like it one bit."

"I don't think I like it either," Kent admitted. "Who all have you told?"

"You're the first, and I'm going to ask that you keep this confidential. I hate to worry the whole department until it's absolutely necessary."

"The hell you say!" Kent responded with considerable heat, "Why did you pick me to unload on? Am I a candidate for that ten percent?"

"Not at this point," Marv blushed guiltily. "You're my lead man, but it could include you, or me."

"I've been in this department for better than twenty years and worked hard at my job. I've never had to back up to the pay table since I hired on. Are you telling me that my job is playing out?" Kent lit another cigarette, took a draw and placed it beside his first, which was still smoking. He stubbed it out and stared at Marv Freeman.

It was true that Kent had twenty years employment at TLC. He'd been hired immediately after graduating high school, and the company had tailored his education with specialized courses to sharpen his skills in sales promotion and keeping customers happy. He had excelled in both facets, mainly because people liked him immediately. Most of his customers had become friends, and even the minority who did not like him considered him to be honest.

Kent had worked through the ranks, from trainee to Senior Customer Service Representative. He drew a living wage, had an expense account and a compact company car. His dues to the Lion's Club were paid by the company and he had endured to the plateau of four weeks paid vacation.

"Jim Sloan is almost sixty five," Marv continued. "He'll count as half our mandated reduction, but that still leaves us one short. Since you rank second to Jim in years of service, I wanted you to be the first to know."

"Is this a company wide deal?" Kent asked, "or just our department?"

"It's company wide," Marv said. "With one notable exception. The engineering and construction departments are scheduled to increase their numbers. TLC is about to expand facilities and encompass a much larger service area. Our scheduled construction will see erection of 345KV lines over our entire system and we're going to build a nuclear generating plant. Our major undertaking, for the foreseeable future, will be expansion and beefed up transmission and distribution facilities."

"Hold it right there Mr. Freeman," Kent said. "I'm not going to climb around on those steel towers. I don't know how to operate any of that heavy machinery and I don't even want to get close to a nuclear generating plant. If you're priming yourself to ask me to put in an application for a transfer to Engineering, you're barking up the wrong tree. I'd rather read meters or draw unemployment!"

"Now Kent, don't get all hot and bothered. I'm not trying to push you into anything at this stage of the game. All I'm trying to do is keep you advised on what kind of problems we're up against. The 'prestigious jobs and non productive occupations' are drawing criticism from the brass and they're determined to play hell with our way of life! If I knew a way I'd jump ship and swim to Engineering. I'd do it, but they won't let me. I'm their designated hatchet man and through me they're gonna wipe out our entire operation in the sweet by and by. We're selling all the energy we can generate, and on the brink of not giving a hoot in hell about customer relations, or promotions."

Both men cooled to room temperature as Kent lit one more smoke and waited for a signal that the meeting was at an end. When Marv began to paw through the accumulation of memos and correspondence in his incoming box Kent took that as a sign to go. He left Marv's office, and did not even pause at his own desk. He left the building, got into his car and gave himself the rest of the day off. He drove the twenty miles to his rural home and worked in his vegetable garden until sundown.

"Didn't I get enough salt and pepper on your eggs?" Lilly asked. "You've just picked at your breakfast, and you've already smoked five cigarettes. Are you sick—or is something bothering you?"

"I'm just a little under the weather," Kent confessed. "I'm going to call in sick and take it easy today. I'll be okay by tomorrow. Didn't get much rest last night. Probably a sinus infection."

"I need to go to the office," Lilly said. "I've got an appointment to show two houses today, but I'll stay home if you need me."

"You go on to work. I'll be fine. And thanks for the breakfast—it was great. I'll see you when you get in this evening." When he heard Lilly start her car Kent called the office and told June that he'd not be coming in. "Upset stomach," was the way Kent explained it. He opened a fresh pack of cigarettes and settled into his recliner for some serious thought, and old western movie reruns.

Chapter III

J.B. Clemons always arrived at the office early. He told his secretary Sally that he liked to do his paper work before the workday got too hectic. In actuality J.B., or Bill as he was known around Ringer, hated paper work. Sally, who had been secretary ten years longer than J.B. had been local manager in the fading oil town of Ringer, actually ran the office. J.B. knew it, Sally knew it, J.B.'s wife Florence knew it and unfortunately J.B.'s superior over at Oak Grove knew it.

John Darby had the dubious distinction of being TLC's Division Manager of a five county area that had been in steady decline since WW II. In addition to Division Headquarters at Oak Grove, John also had five local offices as his responsibility. They were located in the crossroads towns of Bo Dark, Morgan, Chocktaw, Hilton and Ringer. John Darby had a force of sixteen employees at headquarters and three at most of his outposts. Each local office featured a local manager, a secretary and a service man with a pickup truck. All, that is, excepting Ringer. Ringer was the least populated and was located only eight miles east of Oak Grove. Maintenance was done by Sam Barnes, who worked out of Oak Grove.

When John got word that he was to jettison one of his outposts he was not surprised. TLC was in the paring down process and rumors of Ringer's closing had preceded official notification by thirty days.

"What will I do with Clemons and Sally Upshaw?" Darby queried when Dill Scratch, V.P. of Operations, appeared at his office with the official word.

"John," Dill looked at him with an unwavering stare, "you'll do what is necessary. You are our Division Manager and we respect your judgment in this matter. We're awash in superfluous employees who perform marginal, unnecessary jobs in outdated and stagnant locations. The Ringer local office has outlived its usefulness, and you and I both know it. The office rent and salaries for two employees exceeds our revenue each and every month and," he added, "Ringer is only the first to go. In due time the other four local offices in your division will be shut down. All division operations will be handled out of Oak Grove with you in control."

The ax had fallen and John Darby's only comfort was the prospect that he would still have a job when the blood letting was over. Secretly, he relished the opportunity to rid himself of local Manager J.B. Clemens, Sally Upshaw and the TLC office in Ringer, Texas. John followed two steps behind and stood attentively as Scratch seated himself in the sleek Roadmaster Buick.

"When should I begin the operation?" John asked timidly as Scratch reached for the door pull. Scratch looked at his watch.

"It's three in the afternoon," He stated, "Why don't you wait until eight o'clock in the morning? That way you'll have time to plan how you're going to handle it." The Vice Presidential Buick backed from the curb and pulled away from Oak Grove Divisional Headquarters.

J.B.'s early morning paperwork consisted of a cursory glance at the Metroplex Star Telegram and the avid reading of the sport and comic sections. Then, J.B. would get a half dozen sheets of company stationery and run them, one by one, through the paper shredder on the corner of his desk. Next he'd refold and place the newspaper on Sally's desk along with a handwritten note explaining that he would be away from the office on business until around noon. That done, he would climb into his compact two door Chevy and make a bee line for the Ringer Municipal Golf Course. Dusty Lane, Ringer's wheeler-dealer independent oil producer would be waiting, with a cooler full of Rocky Mountain Beer positioned on his golf cart.

Dusty was heir to a sizable fortune which had been amassed by his father, Rusty, during the boom days of Ringer. Rusty had accumulated mineral rights to most of the county before exploration and production of the shallow pools was even a dream. He had profited mightily, saved scrupulously and died at an early age. Young Dusty had lived high on the hog and had gone through five wives before his fortieth birthday. He'd also expended a considerable sum of money during the process, but his stripper wells still operated around the clock and Dusty had a trusted and honest manager for his oil business, who looked out for the day-to-day operations of the Dusty Lane Oil and Exploration Company. Dusty, also owned Ringer's only bank.

When wife number five left Dusty he consoled himself with a new hobby. He took up golf. He played a round each and every morning, and he always played with Bill Clemons. It was a ritual of ten year's standing.

"Usual stakes?" Bill popped the top on a frosted can.

"Usual stakes," Dusty responded.

chapter IV

Jimmy John Tolliver entered the break room at precisely 7:30 A.M. His arrival time never varied by sixty seconds, according to Roberta Mullins. He strode around the room and performed his visual inspection as Roberta put the finishing touches to the forty tables. She had to put the chairs back in place most every morning so that there were four at each chromed table, and that was what she was doing when J.J. entered.

"Good morning Roberta, am I late?"

"No sir, Mr. Tolliver," Roberta forced a smile, "you're right on time!" The exchange was a daily ritual, and as far as Roberta was concerned, an interruption to her chores. She'd heard the elevator door operate.

He traveled his usual route, peering at the transparent gauges of the sparkling coffee urns and hefting the sugar and cream pillow baskets for weight. The swizzle stick disbursements were scanned, the napkin dispensers were hand squeezed by J.J. to satisfy himself that they were properly filled, and each ashtray received a cursory inspection for cleanliness.

Next, J.J. wordlessly proceeded to each vending machine to satisfy himself that they were filled to capacity for the morning run. Then he produced his key ring, entered his private office and brought out the four honor system slot boxes which he placed at their appointed sites around the four sided coffee island. Roberta watched wordlessly and braced herself for the inevitable revelation that she'd overlooked one minor detail. She knew what it would be, since she always left an easily discoverable flaw for J.J. to find. It had not taken her long to perfect this strategy when Mr. Tolliver had come on board. He was going to discover a shortcoming. He'd never failed to come up with one in his ten years as Employee Benefits Coordinator.

"Roberta," he said, "you missed one side of the napkin dispenser on table four. You'll need to take care of that. Otherwise, the place is in top notch condition."

"Yes sir," Roberta responded as she opened a drawer and got the sheaf of napkins she'd put there. "I must have been distracted by something. I'm glad you found it. Thanks."

"No harm done," J.J. chuckled. "Two heads are better than one! We're a good team and I'm always pleased with your job performance." As Roberta walked to table four, he drew himself a steaming cup of decaf and went to his favorite table, where there was no ashtray. He had a low opinion of cigarettes, and cigarette smokers, and if he had his way there'd be no smoking in his break room.

Placement of the honor system coin boxes allowed him unobstructed vision of all four. He also had a low opinion of anyone who failed to deposit full payment for coffee. Admittedly, sometimes when a crowd accumulated he could not always be certain that everyone paid, but he had keen hearing and eagle vision. Not often did TLC lose money on coffee sales. J.J. was a contented man and well qualified for his job.

Attorney Lyndon Moon was normally the first customer unless he was out of town attending to legal matters. J.J. cherished Lyndon's absence. When the councilor was in town he usually made his arrival a full fifteen minutes before the flood of employees at eight o'clock. Regular coffee shop opening time was 7:30, and trade was always brisk from secretaries who took a cup of coffee and a snack to their workstations.

Department heads were exempt from being prompt at their work place, since they needed to touch base with each other and discuss work in progress. In truth, it is doubtful that company business was even in the top ten most popular subjects. Football and baseball games were dissected and examined in detail, the woeful shortage of competent employees and the heavy labor burden being imposed upon supervisors were the main topics, until a gradual erosion of supervisors migrated to their jobs by ascending rank. "The biggest wheels always roll out last," was the way Roberta put it.

Lyndon Moon ranked above all the "Big Wheels" who peopled the lower nine floors of the Corporate Offices of TLC and was often still sipping his coffee and puffing cigarettes when the last of the stragglers departed. His office was, after all, on the tenth floor alongside the many VPs and President and General Manager Vernon Marmaduke. Lyndon was not greatly revered on either floor, but in his role as staff attorney he enjoyed an almost legendary niche in the organization. He knew the exact location of the closets, which housed the skeletons accumulated by the ruling hierarchy of TLC, and he had an extensive rap sheet and running tab on the heirs apparent who were advancing toward the coveted positions on the tenth floor. It was a wise decision to court favor with Lyndon Moon—and keep a wary eye upon him.

J.J. Tolliver went the extra mile in maintaining a tranquil relationship with Lyndon Moon, since he could not weather any tempest Lyndon might spawn upstairs. In his monthly statement, which was forwarded to Vernon Marmaduke, he had never made mention of Lyndon Moon's irritating practice of thumping the honor box in lieu of depositing coins. It was a wise decision. J.J. knew that Lyndon was the ultimate recipient of his "dead beat" report. He'd been told that President Marmaduke didn't even bother to look inside the envelope at his report. Instead, according to an unimpeachable source, he submitted it to the company lawyer, Lyndon Moon.

Once Lyndon mercifully departed, J.J. put his and Lyndon's cups in the trash receptacle and went into his office as Roberta began her sprucing up in preparation for the 9:30 run, which actually began around nine and lasted until eleven.

J.J. seated himself at his desk and unlocked the drawer safe. He poured yesterday's collection of money onto his desktop and began his coin rolling operation. He did not hurry the task. As a matter of fact, he examined each coin's date and mintmark as he prepared them for encasement in the paper sleeves.

An untrained observer might conclude that he was a coin collector, but that conclusion would be an error. J.J. knew the going price for scarce coinage, and when he ran across a rare or semi-rare specimen he would cull it out and replace it with one from his pocket. Once a week he made a trip to the Cow Town coin shop up the street and sold his finds. His big discovery of all time was a 1909 S VDB Lincoln Head Cent. It had appraised at one hundred and sixty five dollars. It had also sold for that amount.

"That coin has a very fine grade," Mr. Ryan had told J.J. "I'll bet it's been in someone's collection for years. Probably spent by accident."

"Could have been," J.J. admitted, "I got it in change at a garage sale I think."

He was interrupted by his telephone and after allowing two rings he picked up the receiver "J.J. Tolliver—Employee Benefits" he said in his most professional voice.

"J.J., Betty Gimble. Mr. Marmaduke has requested your presence in his office at eleven. Is there any reason why you cannot make it?" Betty was Mr. Marmaduke's personal secretary and J.J. often visited with her when she was on coffee break. In his estimation he and Betty were on an equal plane of importance, since they both reported directly to Vernon Marmaduke.

"I'll be there! Do you have any idea why Mr. M wants to see me?" J.J. asked. "Did he ask me to bring anything?"

"No idea," Betty said, "just be here—and don't be late."

Chapter V

Goose Kelly lifted the screen door so that it would not drag, pushed it open and faced the blinding glare of the rising sun. He shaded his eyes with a bandaged right hand.

He was outfitted in a pair of faded denims, a grimy T-shirt and mismatched socks. His sparse halo of hair was uncombed and he had been conserving razor blades for a good spell of time.

"Who's here?" He called out again. Under his breath Ben swore an oath at Goose's presence and his lost breakfast break in Carlsbad.

"You still got that biting dog?" Ben turned back toward the house.

"Who in hell are you? And what do you want?" Goose answered one question with two of his own.

"Ben Drill! I work for the Light Company. Been a while since I've been here, but I need to visit with you if you've got the time."

"You're that land buyer ain't you?" Goose said as he released the screen door. It sagged to the floor and stopped. He lifted it and urged it shut.

"Yessir," Ben admitted. "We traded on two miles of right of way a few years back. I need to talk to you again."

"About another damn electric line?"

"Maybe." Goose stood and thought the request over. Ben stood his ground but made no motion to approach the house.

"You still got that dog?"

"I can't hear you real good," Goose said. "You might as well come up here on the gallery. Can't hardly see you neither."

"Where's your dog?" Ben asked again as he climbed the steps. "Is he under the porch?"

"Naw", Goose sat heavily in a straight back, binder twine bottomed chair. "He took up with a bitch coyote here awhile back and he don't come around these days. Hated to lose Moose to a bitch coyote, but that's the way a dog will treat a man sometimes. Some women will quit on you like that too."

"Hate to hear it," Ben lied, "He'll most likely be coming back one of these days though. He'll realize how good he had it and come slinking back with his tail between his legs."

"Hope so," Goose said. "Take a seat on that nail keg and we'll talk. But I'll tell you right off—I don't need no more damn electrical lines on this place! It looks like a jungle of pine tree stobs already. The oil companies and the electric companies has ruint this ranch. Damn oil wells, pipelines and electric lines all over the whole shebang. I can't pasture two cows to the section these days."

Pete "Goose" Kelly was the outright owner of 51% of the Kelly Ranch and the petroleum that was pooled beneath the two hundred-section expanse of scrub mesquite and blow sand. His three brothers and two sisters shared equally in the remaining 49%. They were scattered across a goodly portion of the world, and living handsomely on their fractions of the royalty checks.

Sam and Sarah Kelly had migrated west from Alabama in 1875. They were bound for California, but they only managed to get a little past the halfway mark between Metroplex and El Paso. Their narrow wheeled wagon had difficulty on a particularly treacherous expanse of sand and old Blue's heart had burst trying to best that sand. Red was the surviving member of the team, but it was unreasonable to expect him to pull the wagon to California by himself, so Sam and Sarah altered their plans. They built a canvas-topped dugout and became the first citizens of Badger, Texas. Sam put their meager nest egg into land and he and Sally set about the production of children. They ceased operations when the number reached a half dozen. Goose was the last. His Christian name was Peter but daddy Sam had bestowed the nickname "Goose" on him. "He wakes up in a new world every morning," Sam told Sarah.

Sam's appraisal may, or may not, have been on the mark, but his son Goose was the only child who did not graduate Texas Tech, in Lubbock, with a degree. Goose barely managed to finish high school, and although he enrolled at the Red Raider Institution of higher learning on an athletic scholarship, he only lasted one semester. He came home to mama and daddy, and his education was pronounced as complete. He stayed around the home place and was rewarded for his presence. To the chagrin of his brothers and sisters the terms of the will put

Pete in the driver's seat. When the will was read the educated Kelly children's wailing and gnashing of teeth was heard throughout the Permian Basin. But to no avail. Their unified contention that brother Pete was non compos mentis was lustily disputed and disproved in court by Christopher Finn. He followed Sam and Sarah's directives to the letter, making sure that Pete came out on top. Attorney Finn had also profited mightily for his defense and representation of Pete "Goose" Kelly.

"You can all go to hell, or back to wherever you hang your hat," was the way Christopher defended the final distribution of assets. "Peter stood by his parents until they went away, and they engaged me to see that he be awarded controlling interest in the Kelly Ranch."

Molly, Peggy, Paul, Brian, and Robert opted to go back to their homes, in lieu of going to hell, and they promptly received their proportionate share of oil revenue that poured into the office of CPA Warren Barnett of Vast Plain. Mr. Barnett acted as financial trustee in the collection and doling out of the royalty income.

Attorney Finn and accountant Barnett shared a legendary dislike for each other and that fact was precisely why Sam Kelly had engaged them to see to Pete's welfare. "They won't buddy up and try to cheat my boy", was the way he put it. "They'll watch each other like chicken hawks." The passage of time had proven the wisdom of Sam Kelly.

As additional compensation for their talents and diligence Christopher Finn and Warren Barnett had gained area wide recognition and now represented landowners from all around the Permian Basin. Their mistrust of each other had endured for forty years. Rarely had either lost a client, and no client had ever lost a dime. An unlikely but successful team.

It had been 1940 when Sam and Sarah Kelly had gone to their eternal reward. They were returning from a trip to the Piggly Wiggly Store over in Pasos, when their earthly existence came to an abrupt ending. Their crossing of the railroad in Badger was intersected broadside by a sixty-car train bound for El Paso, and running late.

"How'd you hurt that hand?" Ben could not keep his eyes from the ham caliber, wrapped and duct taped right hand that Goose cradled with his left.

"Got bit by a rattler," Goose unwrapped the length of cotton sock. "It really puffed up on me. Don't reckon he'd struck anything in a good while and was packing a full tank of poison I guess. Anyways, it swole up to the size of a football. It's been a week, and it still throbs a good deal at night." Goose's fingers stuck out like teats on a cow's udder and from the elbow down his arm was an angry purple. Ben could see that the fang marks were about two inches apart, and he judged that the rattlesnake had been full grown. He wondered whether the snake had survived.

"How'd it happen?" Ben asked. "He didn't get you up here on the gallery did he?" He looked around with some alarm at the accumulation of buckets, coils of rope and a couple of old saddles.

"Naw, I got a patch of early butter beans out in the back yard and the blamed things clumb up in the mesquite shinnery like morning glories. They get a good watering most every day and that old snake was laid up in the shade while I was picking a mess. He nailed me a good lick. For all I know, he might like butter beans."

"Did you kill him?" Ben was keenly interested in that snake, as he continued his inspection of the littered porch.

"Naw, when I got him shook loose he struck out and darted under the house. I was so surprised I couldn't find a plank to brain him with. Then, I had to find a can of coal oil to soak my hand and draw the poison. It'll be all right inside of another week and then me and brother snake is going to come to an understanding. If that damn Moose hadn't been off courting that bitch coyote he'd a killed that rattler," he sighed.

The conversation wandered aimlessly for better than an hour before Goose asked the reason for the visit. Ben acted as though he'd completely forgotten why he was there as he shifted his position on the nail keg. The top was recessed a half inch below the ring of stave ends and they were sharp enough to be uncomfortable.

He told Goose that a major sulfur plant was under construction twenty miles to the west. TLC had been asked to construct a 345KV transmission line and one of the routes crossed a portion of the Kelly Ranch. Ben could have been more specific and told Goose that the actual crossing was decided, but he didn't feel it was in the best interest of negotiations to furnish all the details, nor to show the aerial photographs which were safely locked in the trunk of his car. Thirty-five years on the job had taught Ben patience—and to never show his hole card on the first contact. Unless the client desperately needed money. Goose Kelly did not need money.

Goose voiced his objection to the project and suggested that the line be put on somebody else's place, on railroad right of way, or on the median strip of the US Highway. Both, Pete pointed out, ran to the Del Ray country and those strips of land were already cluttered.

Ben assured Goose that those routes were under consideration by the TLC engineering department as well as two others. He cited friendship as his reason for coming to see Goose first, so that he would have sufficient time to think about the project while the final decision was pending. Just in case the railroad and the Interstate Highway turned TLC down, which they'd do if they were asked. They always had, so they would not be approached.

Goose said he appreciated the information and thanked Ben for coming by to alert him, and reiterated that he had all the electric lines he wanted.

"I about half way agree with you Mr. Kelly," Ben said, "but you can't produce oil without electricity and pipe lines. And, like they say in the papers, 'we can't stand in the way of progress!' I just want you to think about the possibility of selling us the right of way for a line, while our engineers are doing their planning. They know where the line has to begin and where it has to end. What they've got to figure out is how to get there."

"I hate them creosote poles all over the place," Goose said. "They bleed that tar into the ground and it kills all the grass. Cows can't last without vegetation to eat!"

Ben explained that the proposed facility would not be wooden. Instead it would be steel towers and spaced to span a mile with only five supports. Therefore, the line would not be such an impediment to the land, and with each tower being four legged, cattle found them handy for scratching their backs. The bottom brace is at an angle that cows and horses of any height can use as a tick scraper. For that reason alone, Ben pointed out, such facilities were prized by fortunate farmers and ranchers who already enjoyed such a line.

"You're full of crap Mr. Drill," Goose smiled. "Do you peddle ice boxes to Eskimos too?"

"I'm not telling you that our route will cross your ranch Mr. Kelly. What I'm saying is, I value your friendship and I just wanted you to be the first man in the county to know what could be coming this way. I'd appreciate your keeping it confidential until I get back to you in the next few days. By then I should have a set of aerial photos, a map and a picture of the transmission towers."

Goose Kelly vowed his silence, which meant that every landowner in the area would know about it before sundown. Exactly what Ben wanted. He was not new at the game, and had the scars to prove it, but he collected a lot fewer scars nowadays than he had back in his youth.

"I guess I should be getting on down the road," he rose, arched his back inward and stuck out his hand. Goose extended his good left hand, but did not get up from his chair.

"Sure hope that hand gets better," Ben said, "and I hope old Moose comes home."

"Thanks," Goose said, "but before you get away let me slip on my boots, and we'll go out back and pick you a mess of butter beans."

Chapter VI

Jimmy John Tolliver gave his shoes a good buffing, straightened his narrow conservative belt so that the buckle was positioned directly atop his belly button, and centered the knot in his tie to the inverted vee formed by his button down collar. He inspected his thinning hair, positioned it for best coverage of his balding spot and sprayed two liberal bursts of breath enhancer into his mouth. He was standing before Betty Gimble's desk at precisely 10:50 A.M.

"J. J. Tolliver reporting for duty," he clicked his heels and snapped to mock attention.

"Go on in. Mr. Marmaduke is expecting you," Betty did not even look up from her work.

"Good morning Mr. Marmaduke," J. J. said. "My father-in-law Sid asked me to pass along his best wishes when we talked last weekend. He just wanted you to know that he's enjoying his retirement down in Galveston, but he still misses his work here at TLC."

Vernon Marmaduke removed his feet from the corner of his desk and motioned for J. J. to be seated. He finished his fingernail cleaning and put his letter opener in his middle desk drawer.

Sidney Partain had never been, and was not now a dear and trusted friend to Vernon Marmaduke, but he had served as Vice President of Employee Benefits for forty years. Sidney had been a V. P. when Vernon was hired and he had remained in that position until his mandatory retirement six months ago. Sidney had seen to J. J.'s advancement to his present position as Employee Benefits Co-Ordinator. J. J.'s chief qualification was that he was Sidney's son-in-law and husband to daughter Nancy.

"Next time you talk to Sid, you tell him we still miss him. I'm glad he's having a good life and enjoying retirement. He earned it with his forty year's service," Vernon smiled.

"I'll do that," J.J. settled into the chair. "Now, what can I do for you?"

"Jim, conditions are changing here at TLC," Vernon began. "We are entering a new era with new challenges. Challenge brings change, and that's why I asked you to come up and visit with me. An unparalleled expansion of our service system along with unmerciful scrutiny by the PUC, the State and Federal Governmental bodies are changing the way TLC will have to do business. We are being required to do even more, with fewer employees. Blue-collar workers are the ones who will see us through the crisis, and new demands we are faced with. TLC must have more employees with dirty hands at day's end and fewer wash and wear suit wearers. Do you understand what I'm telling you?"

"Not precisely," J. J. croaked, "but of course I am prepared to do whatever is asked of me. Are you telling me that Roberta must go? If so, I can come to work a little earlier and take sole command of the employee coffee shop. It may be a burden at first, but I know that I can satisfactorily muster the energy necessary to maintain the excellence of the employee lounge!"

Patiently, and with suppressed glee Vernon Marmaduke explained that Roberta was not leaving—but Jimmy John Tolliver was being transferred to a new line of work. The work would be radically different, but J. J. was assured that he was qualified and equal to the challenge. The classification and duties would be demanding, but the rewards could be great with the passage of time. J. J. was but forty-five and that left him twenty years to learn and prosper in a new and dynamic vocation. J. J. sat wordlessly but he could feel the beads of sweat on his brow. He could not think of anything to say, so he sat numbly and did not speak for what seemed an eternity.

"Exactly what will I be doing?" he found his voice as Vernon stared at him without expression. "And when do I start?"

"This is not the time to go into details," Vernon said. "You'll hear from me through Mrs. Gimble before the week is out. In the meantime I'd appreciate your keeping our chat confidential. Just rest assured that what is coming is good for you and TLC. That will be all for now, but you be sure and give my best to Sid next time you two make connections."

J. J. managed to get his legs under himself and walked stiffly to the door and let himself out. His mouth was dry and his heart's tempo was rapid and audible—at least to J. J.

"Come back and see us." Betty smiled as he made his way into the hall and punched the down elevator button.

chapter VII

Butter beans ranked low on the list of things Ben needed to make his life complete and he did his best to politely refuse the charity of Goose Kelly.

"I don't want to run you short on butter beans Mr. Kelly," Ben said as his eyes grew accustomed to the unlit interior. "Besides that, you need to take good care of that hand. Picking butter beans might be about the worst thing you can do with a hurt hand."

"These are speckled butter beans," Goose seemed not to hear. "Big as silver dollars and with a flavor that will knock your boots off. You like butter beans don't you?" He located his boots and climbed into a giant shiny barber's chair. An identical chair was across the room and Ben seated himself. The chairs had not been there the last time he was in the Kelly place, but they did not surprise him. Framed photographs of Goose's parents, Sam and Sarah, which were prominently centered on a wall, were what always drew Ben's attention. The photographs were of Pete's folks as they lay in their caskets awaiting burial. Those photographs always gave Ben the willies, but he could not avoid looking at them. Twin barber chairs paled in the company of those portraits.

"Boy, this is one comfortable seat," he said as Goose smiled appreciatively, "where'd you get these chairs?"

"Swapped for them," Goose said, "I wish I had another one or two. You can rear 'em back, spin 'em around and make them go up and down. I got rid of my couch so I'd have plenty of room to operate them in!" He pulled his boots on and they went through the kitchen, where Pete located a large paper sack, and then into the back yard.

Ben could scarcely believe his eyes when he saw the butter bean growth. They vines covered the ground to knee depth and covered all the limbs of several twelve to fifteen foot mesquite saplings. Butter beans hung in grapelike clusters and there were enough of them to feed a battalion. "Damn," Ben said, "I ain't never seen such a crop of speckled butter beans! And this early in the year too."

"I doped them with a pickup load of cow manure," Goose said, "and I water them every evening. I kinda like you, so I want you to have a bate of good butter beans!"

"Well, I'll be much obliged," Ben said "I'll shell them out tonight and get my wife to cook them. She's really going to be surprised," He was not stretching the truth with his statement. Flossie would not only be surprised—she'd likely refuse to cook them and deposit them in a trash bag. Flossie did not cook butter beans, turnips, cabbage or catfish in her kitchen. She said that she didn't like to stink up the house.

Ben offered to do the picking, but Goose would not allow it. "You hold the sack, and I'll do the picking. Can't set that sack on the ground. It will get wet and the bottom will fall out. It won't take me long to pull you a mess—I've had lots of experience at picking butter beans and I can do it without hurting the vines."

Wordlessly Ben held the bag as Goose went into action. He used his bandaged hand to brace the vine as he plucked the bean clusters. In a matter of minutes he had filled the bag to the halfway mark and Ben urged him to call it a mess. "That'll keep me hulling beans until midnight," was the way he put it. Finally, as a last resort he squeezed the bag closed and declared that he had enough butter beans for his whole neighborhood.

"Open up that sack," Goose laughed, "I got to put one more handful in for good measure." He reached for that last handful, and stood on tiptoes to grasp a pineapple size cluster of pods.

That was when the snake struck his outstretched hand. They backed away hastily, but Goose brought the snake with him. Ben gave them negotiating room as he looked for a club. He dropped his sack of beans and picked up a gooseneck hoe as Goose managed to extract his hand from the rattler's fangs. He was swearing in loud and vivid volume as the snake fell into the vines and vanished.

"Cut him off at that crawl space!" Goose screamed. "He's making a break to get under the floor. He's the same one that nailed me last time!"

Ben hurried to the opening as Goose cursed and stomped among the vines to speed the rattler's journey. When the snake emerged from cover Ben took his head off with one quick and decisive blow. He also broke the hoe handle. Goose sucked the venom from the two punctures and spit it to the ground.

"You got in a good lick on that sucker Mr. Drill, and I'm in your debt. I'll hang him on the fence directly and maybe we'll get a little rain. Now, pick up your sack of beans and we'll go back around to the front gallery. I've got a can of coal oil out there for doctoring purposes."

Ben gingerly retrieved his bag of speckled butter beans and followed Goose to the front porch. He did his best to persuade Goose to go to the emergency room at Medical Center. "I'll drive you over and bring you back home Mr. Kelly," he said, but Goose submerged his hand in a five gallon bucket of kerosene and assured Ben there was no need to go to any hospital.

"He ain't had time to build up a potent dose like he had last time," Goose said. "That old rattler shore messed up biting me while I had somebody around to chop off his head. If old Moose wasn't out chasing around with a bitch coyote he'd a got him last time and I wouldn't have got bit again. This coal oil will take care of everything, and you took care of that old rattler. Don't you even worry about that hoe handle you broke."

Ben sat for an hour or better while Goose soaked his hand. He hesitated to drive away and leave a snake bit man to die on his front porch. To pass the time he shelled his butter beans and made conversation to keep Goose conscious. Goose remained coherent and occasionally he would lift his arm and inspect his stricken hand. It was not swelling up to the size of the wrapped one, and Ben began to feel that he was concerning himself with a situation that was not his business.

"Well, Mr. Kelly, I believe you're going to tough it out and I guess you know whether you should go to the hospital or not. I hate to desert you, but I need to get on down the road," Ben said. "Sometimes I try to get home for the weekend, but I'll be back this way in a few days to check on your health."

"Everything will be O.K.," Goose assured him. "I've been snake bit more times than you got fingers and toes—and I never went to the doctor for any one of them. I'll be fine! I want you to get back soon as you know for sure if the light company wants to build across me. You and me can probably work out a deal to get it done."

Ben threw the hulls in the front yard, walked to his car and put his sack in the front seat. He removed his billfold from his back pocket and put it alongside his butter beans. He started the engine, backed up and turned around. With a final wave he drove away to the east and Vast Plain. It was a quarter to ten and he decided that Furr's Cafeteria would be a good place to catch a meal. He hoped butter beans were on the menu. He craved a helping and he knew that Flossie didn't like to smell up the house with the stink of cooking butter beans

Chapter VIII

"Murphy's Law got us," Wiley Kyle said as he seated himself across from Verne Marmaduke. Dill Scratch occupied a third chair at the well appointed table in the Executive Board Room. Wiley was visibly unnerved as he sugared and creamed his coffee.

"Nothing much to be accomplished by an autopsy," Dill said, "but we've got to pursue measures to correct this situation."

"Trying to fix blame is not the reason for us getting together," Verne stated. "The purpose of this meeting is to fix what's broke. We're facing a construction program that will tax TLC to the marrow and we can't go into battle short handed. Our Right of Way Department fell apart from old age!"

In early June of 1984 Right of Way supervisor Tim Burkeen had barely survived a head on car crash while he and wife Tessie were vacationing in the Houston area. Tim was now in a rest home that he did not know the name of, and passed his time drooling oatmeal on his bib, wetting the bed linens and staring out a window.

That same month Henry "Hank" Brown went Tim Burkeen one better. He was admitted to All Saints Hospital for overnight observation and never lasted the night. Hank was sixty four, with a forty year stretch of right of way negotiation to his credit when he closed his final deal.

Garth Gankle and Ben Drill were two of the pall bearers at Hank's funeral and Garth's employment ended before the month was out. An eagle eyed "Bean Counter" discovered that Garth had achieved his seventieth year and had been a refugee from mandatory retirement for half a decade. The oversight was corrected and Garth was forcibly ousted from the salaried ranks of TLC. Personnel reasoned that Garth had escaped detection due to the rarity of his appearances at the office.

Garth, whose native tongue was profanity loved his job and was not prepared to sit home with his wife Blanch so he signed on with

Global Acquisition as a Senior Right of Way Negotiator and realized a substantial increase in salary. Coupled with his earned retirement package at TLC, Garth was doing exceptionally well and still on the road. No complaints were forthcoming from Blanch.

Benjamin Arthur Drill was the sole survivor in the right of way acquisition forces of TLC when April 1984 drew its first warm breath, and he fell heir to the unfinished projects near High Bank, where Hank had been working, and Garth's 138KV tap line down in the Whitlow area. Of course he was still expected to acquire rights for construction of the 345KV facility in far western Texas. He did not complain although his work stations formed a tree hundred mile, triangle sided stretch of real estate. He plied his trade at the same rate as always. He no longer had an immediate supervisor but he stayed in irregular telephone contact with Brad Hare through Brad's secretary, Ruby Jean Bell. Such contacts were rare and under the control of Ben, since he was sole judge of where he would see the sun rise and who would know. Ben's wife Flossie was the only person who was contacted on a nightly basis, but she did not always write that location down, and even when she did she was not always able to locate it if Brad or Ruby inquired.

Vernon Marmaduke, Dill Scratch and Wiley Kyle were in accord that something must be done—and done quickly.

Dill reported that he would be able to produce a group of candidates to shore up the right of way agent pool within a short time. "The men will not be experienced negotiators," he admitted, "but they will have ingredients that appear to be conducive to performance of the job. They will all have years of service and safe driving records. Hopefully they will adapt quickly. Self discipline is the unknown, and I suggest that they answer directly to Ben Drill during their early training phase. He's been around for years and can provide guidance and supervision until these men get their feet on the ground. I'm not at liberty to provide names right now Wiley, but I think you'll to be pleased with my selections. The new supervisor will, of course, be a graduate electrical engineer, but my search for him is not yet complete."

"Brad and I talked with Ben after Tom Burkeen had his car wreck," Wiley said. "We asked him to be interim Right of Way Manager at that time and he said he'd rather be in hell with his back broke. He has no ambition to supervise and even less desire to perform an office job. I don't know if we can count on him to cooperate in training new right of way agents."

"I hired Ben right after he was discharged from the Army," Verne Marmaduke stated with a twinkle in his eye. "You let me handle him and we'll not have any problems. I put him in the field as a negotiator."

"I'd forgotten about that," Wiley lied, "but now I do remember when you hired him. There's one other thing. Ben says he's going to retire the day he turns fifty-five. The lifetime insurance, medical policy and retirement are the only reasons he's still on the job. He turns fifty-five in January. That gives us nine months to train a new group of agents."

"We'll see about early retirement," Verne smiled. "You might be surprised at my relationship with Ben Drill, but we won't go into that now. Dill will set a meeting for you and your new agents and we'll get this show on the road. We've got to have land to put our lines on, and the first step will be new agents. And, we must never wind up in a bind like this again!"

"No sir!" Wiley agreed.

"We'll get together next Monday in the Engineering Planning Room Wiley," Dill said. That's all I have for the present." Wiley rose, thanked Verne and Dill, then departed to his fifth floor office. Dill got to his feet, pushed his chair back into place and left without another word.

Verne sipped his coffee.

chapter IX

Ben was in Vast Plain by eleven, and drove directly to Furr's Cafeteria out on the Andress Highway. There was no line to contend with, and that's the way he liked it. He slid his tray along the chrome piping unhurriedly making his selections, and found a booth where no one was likely to spot him. Ben didn't like company when he ate, and he also avoided conversation when he could. He talked for a living, and didn't normally do a lot of idle visiting.

With his hunger satisfied he drove to the Ramada, loaded his belongings and checked for phone messages. Mrs. Ruby Jean Carter had called at nine thirty but Ben did not call back. He paid out, checked out and hit the road for Chalk Draw.

Dawn Miller checked him in at the Remuda Inn and asked how he'd been doing. "Haven't seen you in a while", she said. "Guess you've been busy."

"Kinda." Ben said, "Have things been going to suit you?"

"Are they supposed to?"

"Nope. If I get any calls I'm not here. Don't even ring my phone. I'm going to take a nap, and I can't think of anybody I want to talk to."

"No problem," Dawn smiled. Ben had been a frequent guest for a quarter century, and she knew his ways. He could always hide and heal at the Remuda. She watched as he picked up his key and walked across the parking lot to room 28. His room. TLC had paid for it over the years, but as far as Dawn was concerned Room 28 belonged to Benjamin Arthur Drill. Within thirty minutes he was sound asleep, and Sherlock Holmes could not find him, unless Ben chose to be found. Dawn was a tried and true guardian when it came to the privacy of her guests.

A knock on the door roused him a little after eight. Ben sat up immediately and looked at his watch. He cursed under his breath and acknowledged the knock. "Be right there," he said. There was no response, and he made a trip to the bathroom where he drained his coffee, washed his face, hands and combed his hair. Then he turned on the bedside lamp and opened the door.

"I thought you weren't going to let me in. Just leave me out here where everybody can see me!" Ruby Jean pouted as she entered.

"We'd both probably be a lot better off if I didn't let you in," Ben said as he took her bag.

Ruby Jean Carter was in her mid-thirties. She was married and mother to a seven-year-old daughter. According to Ruby Jean her husband Don was crude, illiterate and did not understand her. As she stood in that room however, Don was back in Metroplex minding daughter Crissie, while Ruby was enroute to Midway to comfort her sick aunt. At least, that's what she'd told Don.

Ben often wondered how he'd let himself get into such a situation. Shacking up with a woman young enough to be his daughter was contrary to all his beliefs. Somehow, he'd gotten himself into a fix and couldn't find a way to get out.

Ruby Jean was a slip of red haired woman who liked lots of makeup, sexy clothing and adventure. Her arrangement with Rocky Rhodes, an up and coming country and western entertainer had gone sour three months ago and Ben Drill had sympathized and comforted her. A bad mistake.

Ruby Jean was twenty years younger than Ben, but she had as much skill in her chosen field as Ben had in negotiating for rights of way. His late life affair had cooled quickly. He rehearsed his speech weekly to bring the affair to an end, but when Ruby Jean showed up he was not able to get it done. He'd always said that sneaking around on a wife was a thing he'd never do. And even if he did it would certainly not be with an employee of TLC.

"You're supposed to be at the office next Monday," Ruby Jean said. Ben was smoking a cigarette as they lay in bed and half watched the Tonight Show. "I'll get to see you then."

"I won't be in town Monday," Ben said. "I've got to be back out here next week. And, to make matters worse, I've got to be down south tomorrow. The building contractor got thrown off the right of way by somebody. I've got to go get them back on the place or the Engineering Department will have fits! I'll be on the road at daylight in the morning."

"What about me?" Ruby Jean pouted. "Can't you get out of going so early?"

"Can't be helped," Ben said. "I don't have any choice. Why am I supposed to be in the office anyway?"

"Well," she snuggled closer, "it's supposed to be top secret, but they're going to put five trainees in the Right of Way Department. Brad told me to let you know. That's why I called the Ramada. Can you guess who's going to train them?"

"It damn sure ain't going to be me!" Ben sat up and lit another smoke. "They can damn well train themselves. Just like I did!"

"This is your chance to be a supervisor Ben," Ruby Jean said. "You might decide to stay until you're sixty five if they make you a supervisor, Brad says."

"The day I turn fifty five I walk out the door," Ben said. "Driving a hundred thousand miles a year and living in motel rooms is beginning to get old, and I wouldn't be President of TLC if I had to sit behind a desk. I'd rather be in hell with my back broke than work eight to five in an office!"

"Don't snap at me," she said as a tear coursed down her cheek. I just want what's best for you. I want to make you happy, and I know I can if you'll give me a chance."

True to his word, Ben dressed noiselessly and left the room in the pre-dawn chill. He paid out and advised Dawn that a lady would be leaving by mid morning. "You'll need to make both beds, if you need to charge extra I'll pay cash."

"Won't be necessary," Dawn smiled. "Same one as last time?" she asked cheerfully. "The little red head?"

"She's a friend," Ben said. "Be nice to her."

chapter X

The meeting was scheduled for 8:30 A.M., but Wylie Kyle had barely unlocked the door at eight when J. J. Tolliver entered. He looked like he'd had a rough weekend, but he greeted Wylie Kyle with all the charm and tact at his muster. He'd not gone by the employee lounge to check on Roberta, and he hoped that she'd keep her mouth shut about the reason for his absence. He'd told her that he had an important meeting, but he feared she knew everything that was going on, and he further felt like she was enjoying his misfortune.

"How's Mr. Kyle this morning?" J. J. said.

"Just fine Jim. Yourself? You look bright eyed and bushy tailed. I appreciate your taking time to come by. I hope you got the packet through inter-office and had time to look the material over," Wiley paused. Before he could continue J. J. held the manila envelope up for viewing.

"Yessir," he said, "and after careful inspection of these documents I have several questions. I talked by phone to Sid Partain down in Galveston—he's my father-in-law—but he doesn't know a great deal about this particular branch of company operations. When I told him that you asked me to this meeting he asked that I pass along his regards to you and your family. And to tell you how much he's enjoying retirement."

"Good to hear from Mr. Partain," Wiley said. "There will be others joining us in the next few minutes and we'll address any and all questions at that time. We've got coffee and donuts for refreshments." Wiley ladeled coffee into the filter of the five gallon urn and flipped the switch. As the coffee maker began to gurgle he flipped the lids on the donut boxes and set out cups, spoons, cream and sugar. Then he arranged his papers and went into the restroom. "Be right back," he said. J. J. seated himself in a position just around the table corner, opened his packet of papers and his stenographer's spiral notebook. He checked his pocket to be sure that he'd brought his pencil.

Wiley Kyle took his time in the restroom. Time enough to get his temper under control. He listened intently for another arrival, and recalled the last time he'd seen V. P. Sidney Partain, and that recollection was not pleasant.

Sidney Partain's negative vote was the one that had kept him from rising to the V.P. level at TLC. He had watched Dill Scratch claim the chair and position that he deserved. He pulled off three pages of hand wipe and gratefully heard the outside door open and close. He emerged to see Dill Scratch placing his papers at the opposite end of the table, and then three other men come in. Wiley had seen them in the coffee shop, but he did not know their names. He welcomed them and invited them to pour coffee and have a donut. "We're expecting two more," he said. "It's still five minutes until we start, and I suspect they'll be along by then."

The men filled their cups and shook hands all around as they found chairs to their liking. Eight thirty arrived, and the group was still two short of the expected attendees. Dill glanced at his watch and tried to conceal his annoyance. Wiley Kyle tried to appear calm and hide his indignation.

J. B. Clemons opened the door a crack and peered inside. He'd been on the road since six and the rush hour traffic had caused him to be late and had rattled his composure.

"Thank goodness," he said when he recognized Dill Scratch. "I don't get down this way real often and I got lost. I'm sorry for holding the meeting up." He sat down and wiped perspiration from his forehead.

"Get yourself coffee and a donut Bill," Dill said. "We've still got another one to go, so you've not held up anything. It's good of you to come."

Nine o'clock arrived and Dill grew more agitated with each passing moment. He finished his second cup of coffee and called the meeting to order.

"We will not wait any longer," he said," we'll start the meeting. If and when our late-comer arrives Mr. Kyle can brief him on what he's missed." The group fell silent and all eyes were focused on V. P. Dill Scratch as he stood and looked intently at one and all.

"My name is Dill Scratch. I am Vice President of Engineering and Construction. As all of you have been informed, our company is embarking on projects that require additional specialists. The transmission and substation construction forces are under the gun with much to be accomplished in a short time in order to fulfill our commitments to the public and our stockholders.

"Our Right of Way Department, due to unforeseen circumstances, is in desperate need of negotiators. Before any construction is possible we must have land. That's where you men can better yourselves and provide a needed service. You've been hand picked from other branches of the company, and you have impeccable service records and the wholehearted recommendation of your supervisors.

At this juncture I'd like each of you to introduce yourself, beginning on my left, and going clockwise around the table. Please state your name, your position and years of service at TLC." Dill called on J. B. Clemons who immediately regretted his choice of chairs, but he rose to his feet and looked up and down the table at the five men who were eyeing him. He cleared his throat and stared fixedly at the tabletop.

"I'm J. B. Clemons. Most people call me Bill. I've been working for TLC since my discharge from the Army in 46. I'm past my thirty-fifth anniversary with the company. My wife's name is Florence and we have one daughter who is grown and married. Her name is also Florence and she's going to have a baby in about four months. There's no way I can get out of being a grandpa.

"I was local manager at Ringer for thirty years and have always tried to do a good job, but Ringer's office has closed." J. B. sat down.

"I'm Harold Ackers. People call me Hal. I've been in customer service for eight of my eleven years service. I'm forty years old and have a wife and two kids—one of each variety." Hal paused and was pleased to note that everyone, including Dill Scratch, smiled at his analysis.

"I welcome the chance to get into another line of work. Our Customer Service Department is thinning out, and a change of jobs is more to my liking than moving back to Oklahoma."

"Bob Barrick is my name and I'm a year younger than old Harold. We've worked together in customer service for the past eight years or so. I've been at TLC for sixteen years, and I'm not married. I was once, but luckily I am not a daddy and my ex and I still speak to each other." Bob sat down and Wiley Kyle looked to his right. J. J. Tolliver rose to his full five foot six and greeted the assembly.

"J. J. Tolliver here! I've enjoyed twenty-four years of employment at Texas Lighting Company. I have served at several locations and in a variety of roles that I will not go into detail about. Currently, I'm serving as Employee Benefits Co-Ordinator with responsibility for our break room and various other employee benefits. Although I do not know all you gentlemen personally I have seen you from time to time, enjoying the facilities which are provided by TLC. Complaints have been rare during my tenure at our break room location and I'm partially responsible for that. I've enjoyed my work although it is demanding sometimes. Frankly, I'm reluctant to leave my old post, but I know that whatever comes next will be equally rewarding. My wife of many years is the former Nancy Partain. She is the only child of Mr. and Mrs. Sidney Partain. Sid, as I call him was a Vice President here at TLC until his recent retirement. In a recent conversation I mentioned that a possible career change might loom ahead and Sid wished me well and passed his best wishes along to you men as we embark on a new adventure. He also said that he was enjoying his retirement." J. J. paused and glanced around the table and it was apparent that he had not run down. He was licking his lips prepatory for a resumption of testimony when Dill Scratch spoke.

"Thank you Mr. Tolliver", he said. "It would take a long time to hear your whole story, but we're pressed for time and need to move along. We've one other man to hear from, and then we'll move to the second stage of the program which will be in the capable hands of Wiley Kyle. Unfortunately, as much as I'd like to stay, I have responsibilities that I must attend to."

"My name is Kent Fields", Kent rose, "I've been a Customer Service Rep for several years—actually since I graduated high school. I'm married to Lilly—we have a grown son and my boss, Marv Freeman, is my reason for being here today. Thank you!" Kent sat back down.

"With that", Wiley Kyle said, "we'll take a ten minute break and get into for phase two of this session. "I have to get back to my office for a few minutes, so you men can take a restroom break and enjoy more coffee and donuts. We sincerely appreciate your taking the time to come down and get us underway Mr. Scratch. Without men like you TLC would not be the dynamic company it is today."

chapter XI

"Where in hell is Ben?" Wiley asked as he fumed past Ruby Jean's desk and into Brad Hare's office. "I left word last Friday to get him in here for our meeting today! He was due at eight thirty and he still hasn't showed up." Brad looked up from his cluttered desk but Wiley's excited state did not ruffle him. Wiley paced to the window and looked down on Bowie Boulevard as he awaited an answer.

"Ruby, would you come in here for a few moments?" Brad keyed the intercom, sat back and looked at Wiley's backside. Brad had no earthly idea where Ben Drill was, but the fact that he didn't show up for a meeting neither surprised nor alarmed him.

Ruby Jean was the most dependable source of such information, and as often as not that source failed. She stayed in touch with the agents to the best of her ability, but she was never one hundred percent accurate since she had no way of contacting them when they were on the road unless they chose to call in. Hank Brown had always been easiest to keep track of. Garth Gankle ranked second in availability while Ben Drill ranked lowest of all in the "reporting in" category. Hank had died, Garth, had been forced into retirement and Ben was the only agent still functioning. Ruby, entered Brad's office and Wylie turned and awaited an answer.

"I called Ramada Inn at Vast Plain last Friday," she referred to her written call record. "He'd checked out at two thirty and the desk clerk had no idea which way he went. She knew him, but was not asked to make him a reservation. She thought maybe he was on his way home. I called his home and his daughter told me that he was not there and according to her they'd not heard from him. She took my message and promised to have him call. He didn't, and I don't know whether Donna saw him or not. She may have forgotten to tell him—she's a teenager you know."

"Even if she told him he may not have had time to call," Brad said. "After all, we've got construction going down south toward Whitlow and up north around High Bank. Ben is the only agent left and he's spread mighty thin with a lot on his mind. Besides all that, he hates meetings."

"That skinny S.O.B. may hate meetings but I expect him to show up here once in a while" Wiley fumed. "He's always somewhere else when you need him. I guess he learned it from Brown and Gankle. Those three have kept me on the hot seat for ten long years and my patience has worn mighty thin."

"Mine too," Brad admitted," but we've always told them that they can't buy right of way hanging around this office. They took us at our word. Do you want Ruby to see if she can track him down?"

"No, I guess not," Wiley said "If he shows up he shows up. If he don't, I'll get along without him." Ruby smiled and wiggled her way back to her desk, as Wiley's heat waned to room temperature. He went back to the window and stared fixedly at the traffic far below.

"What do you think of the five applicants?" Brad asked as he found his stub of cigar and lit up. "I knew Bill Clemons when I was out in the Western Division, and it's hard for me to picture him as a land buyer. He can get lost on a one-way street. People seemed to like him over at Ringer though, and I guess that's the main qualification. He's kinda like a big old dog that chews things up, but you just can't kick him."

"He was almost late too," Wiley said, "and he looks like to me he's been kicked lately. What has he been doing since he lost his manager position?"

"John's had him going to the Post Office and doing 'step and fetch it' work. He lost his company car, his expense account and his membership at Ringer Municipal Golf Course. I'll bet he tries hard if you give him a chance. Actually, we need all five of them—and we need Ben to teach them the tricks of the trade. Getting him to cooperate may be hard to do," Brad added.

"He'll do it for the old man," Wiley said. "Vern hired him and made him an agent over thirty years ago. One word from him and Ben will teach them to jump through hoops. Vernon Marmaduke is really the only superior Ben will acknowledge in the whole company. That's a fact, and the only reason I haven't fired him."

"He's the best right of way agent this company's ever had," Brad said. "He's only had four or five condemnations since he started buying land.

I don't know how he does it, but he can charm ninety nine percent of the people. When the chips are down I'd put him up against any of 'em!"

"I know," Wiley admitted. "If he walked in now I'd probably forget how damn mad I am."

"Maybe he'll show up or call in yet," Brad said. "We don't know where he is or how to find out." Wiley glanced at his watch and noted that it was time for him to get back to the meeting room. Without another word he left the engineering offices. Ruby smiled as he passed her desk.

chapter XII

Two separate bull sessions were going when Wiley Kiel entered. One included Hal, Bob and Kent. They were in a heated discussion of some of the paper work and sample forms they'd received.

J. J. Tolliver was waxing eloquent for Bill Clemons, who appeared to be searching for an escape route. Wiley knew the feeling and Bill's stock rose in his estimation. Tolliver put his paper work back into his envelope, got up and reclaimed his seat near the head of the table.

"You received a packet of forms representing what this land acquisition game is all about," Wiley said. "You will notice that exhibit "A" is information provided by an abstract company located in the county of the targeted acreage. The current owner, or owners, of the places our line will cross is the important information. That and the aerial photograph attached to it are the tools you will receive once our engineers have settled on a tentative route. That proposed route is marked in heavy line." Tolliver's hand shot into the air. "There'll be time for discussion and questions once we've explored the entire process," He added.

"Next is exhibit "B"—Survey Permission. It's a single page with the land description and location. A space is provided for the signature of the landowner and authorizes a survey team to make a physical center line survey of the proposed crossing. At this point all we are interested in is the feasibility and possibility. If a route is chosen, following a survey, we will negotiate with the landowner for the actual easement.

"Of course, we're already ninety nine percent certain that we have selected the best route for both the company and title holder's convenience.

"We do not pay for this preliminary survey, but we will be scrupulously careful during this phase of route selection. In the event we do any damage, or go a different route, the landowner and the lessee, or tenant if there is one, will be fairly compensated for any damages that might have been done by the survey team.

"Whoever grants survey permission will sign his or her name along with the agent who obtains permission. No notary is necessary. The landowner may keep a copy, but the original must be delivered to Brad Hare, who will see that it reaches the party chief of the survey contractor. The negotiator will also retain a copy, and that copy will prove valuable to him once he is required to go back and negotiate a permanent easement." Wiley paused and poured himself a glass of water. Tolliver timidly raised his hand, and once again was asked to hold his questions. He was assured an opportunity at the end of the session.

"I'll tell you what Mr. Tolliver, I've run out of wind already and since you are fresh and willing to talk, I'm going to ask you to read the fine print on exhibit "C". It is the legal size sheet titled "Easement and Right of Way." There are blank spaces on this exhibit, but when you receive the actual instrument all spaces will be filled with the necessary information. Would you be good enough to do that for me, please?"

"Yes sir Mr. Kiel I'll be happy to help out. Before I begin however I'd like to ask one question and it's important to all of us. We talked about it while we were on break and you were away from the room."

"Fair enough," Wiley said. "What is the question?"

"Are we being offered positions as right of way agents—or are we being interviewed with only a possibility of coming to your department?"

"Each of you has exceeded expectations in your years at TLC. You have been recommended by your supervisors for these positions. By virtue of your presence here you are being offered a new and demanding responsibility in a different line of work. I pledge to each of you that you will be transferred to the Land Acquisition Department and participate as bona fide right of way agents. At present we have but one agent in General Office Engineering, and you men will have the opportunity to try your hands at buying land rights on a three hundred mile 345 KV line which will originate at our Possum Creek Reservoir Generating Station and terminate at Dune Substation, now under construction in Voltaire County. You men will have a week's training to familiarize yourselves with the job requirements. Following that you will be put in the field as right of way negotiators.

"When this meeting concludes each of you will opt to either grasp the opportunity—or go back to your present work station. We are not drafting you—like the Marine Corps, we're looking for a few good men. We believe you five to be good men!

"With that said, I'd like to push on through these exhibits and allow you to learn the rudiments of the job. At day's end I'd like to know your tentative decisions. And—I reiterate—you are not being forced into this. It will be your choice. Once the current project is completed we will make the determination as to whether you are suitable negotiators and you will decide whether or not you are able and willing to continue the job.

"I will not tell you that just anyone can do the work, but I will tell you that I certainly recommend that you take the challenge and give this project your best shot. Right of way buying is a big job, and your future here is assuredly rosier than at the position you now hold.

"Now Mr. Tolliver would you please read the document?" Wiley turned his chair ninety degrees and stared out the window at the sky.

"Easement and Right of Way—State of Texas—County of ____, Know all men by these presents. That ____ of ____ County, Texas, herein, after called "Grantor" whether one or more, for and in consideration of ____ Dollars ($ ____) to Grantor in hand paid by Texas Lighting Company, has granted, sold and conveyed and by these presents does grant, sell and convey unto said company an easement and right-of-way for an electric transmission and distribution line, consisting of a variable number of wires, and all necessary or desirable appurtenances (including towers, H frames or poles made of wood, metal, or other materials, telephone and telegraph wires, guy wires and guy anchorages) at or near the location and along the general course now located and staked out along, over, under, across and upon the following described lines located in ____ County, Texas, more particularly described as follows." J. J. paused for a breath, a sip of water and waited expectantly for whatever remarks might be forthcoming. None were. Kent looked bored, J. B. slumped sadly as though he expected the world to end and Harold and Robert appeared to be asleep. Wiley did not even look around. Tolliver bravely resumed his reading, but his voice had begun to drop in volume and clarity. Wiley was enjoying the erosion immensely.

"Being a strip of land 150 feet wide, being 75 feet on either side of the above described centerline and comprising ____ acres.

"Grantor recognizes that the general course of said line, as above described, is based on preliminary surveys only, and Grantor hereby agrees that the easement hereby granted shall apply to the actual location of said line when constructed.

"Together with the right of ingress and egress over and along the above described right-of-way, and over Grantor's adjacent lands to or from said right-of-way, for the purpose of constructing, operating, improving, reconstructing, repairing, relocating, inspecting, patrolling, maintaining and removing such electric power and communication lines as the Company may from time to time find necessary, convenient or desirable to erect thereon; the right to relocate along the same general direction of said line, the right to relocate said line in the same relative position to any adjacent road if and as such road is widened in the future, the right to lease pole space for the purpose of permitting others to string wire or other desirable appurtenances on said line, the right to remove or prevent the construction on said strip of any or all buildings, structures or other obstructions which, in the sole judgment of the Company, may endanger or interfere with the efficiency, safety, and/or convenient operation of said line and its appurtenances; and the right to trim or cut down trees and shrubbery within, but not limited to, said 150 feet space, to the extent, in the sole judgment of the Company, as may be necessary to prevent possible interference with the operation of said line or to remove possible hazard thereto.

"Grantor reserves the right to use said land for general agricultural and grazing purposes, provided such use shall not include the growing of trees thereon or any other use that might, in the sole judgment of the Company, interfere with the exercise by the Company of the rights hereby granted. Grantor further, reserves the right to lay out, dedicate, construct, maintain and use across said strip such roads, streets, alleys, railroad tracks, underground telephone cables and conduits and gas, water, and sewer pipe lines as will not interfere with Company's use of said land for the purpose aforesaid, provided all such facilities shall be located at angles of not less than 45 degrees to any of Company's lines, and shall be so constructed as to provide with respect to Company's wires and other facilities the minimum clearances provided by law and recognized as standard in the electrical industry. Grantor also reserves the right to erect fences not more than 8 feet high across said land, provided all such fences shall have gates, openings, or removable sections at least 12 feet wide which will permit Company reasonable access to all parts of said land.

"In addition to the consideration above recited for the easement and right-of-way hereby granted, the Company will pay to the owner of the land, and if leased, to his tenant, as they may be respectively entitled, for actual damages done to fences, terraces and growing crops by reason of the construction, maintenance or removal of said line; provided, however, that no such payment will be made for trimming or removal of trees from said land, nor for removal of trees or other obstructions from such 150 foot space after said line is constructed, as hereinabove provided.

"TO HAVE AND TO HOLD the above described easement and rights unto the said Company, its successors and assigns, until said line shall be abandoned, and in that event said easement and right-of-way shall cease and all rights herein granted shall terminate and revert to Grantor, his heirs, successors or assigns; and Grantor hereby binds himself, his heirs and legal representatives, to warrant and forever defend the above described easement and rights unto Company, its successors and assigns, against every person whomsoever lawfully claiming or to claim the same or any part thereof.

"If the construction of the facilities to be erected and located under the terms of this grant is not begun within 15 years from the date hereof this grant shall thereupon terminate and all rights and interests hereunder shall revert to Grantor, his heirs and assigns."

At that point J. J.s voice had faded to an inaudible point, but the audience seemed not to notice. They aroused when the deluge abated, but J. J. licked his lips and continued.

"At the bottom of the document there is a space for the execution date, spaces for the signatures of the land owners and a space designated for the agent's name who secured the easement," J. J. dutifully turned the sheet and inspected the back side.

"On the back," he resumed, "there is a space for notarizing and a _____."

"The rest is self explanatory," Wiley interrupted. "That will be enough for now. As you become more familiar with negotiation everything will fall into place, and it won't sound like Greek or legalese. Right now it's break time. Stretch your legs and get rid of your coffee and we'll wrap this session up, as soon as I can make a brief trip to my office. Thank you very much for reading Mr. Tolliver, and thanks to you others for your attention. Let's take thirty minutes."

"Will we still have time for questions?" J. J. asked.

"All your questions will be answered," Wiley said as he went out the door.

"Man alive," Kent said, "I'm going to the coffee shop for my break. My ears are ringing and Roberta's place is beckoning me." Harold and Bob rose, stretched and fell in behind Kent. Bill, did not relish the prospect of being left in the room with J. J.. He caught them at the elevator.

"What in hell are we getting into?" Harold said. No one answered.

chapter XIII

Wiley spotted him as he passed Brad's office. He made a sharp turn and strode by Ruby Jean's desk without a word. She did not look up from her work, but she knew who was passing, and she smiled.

"Ben, were you aware that you were supposed to be at a meeting at eight thirty this morning?" Wiley was able to keep his temper under control. Ben and Brad were studying a plat, and they looked up at the interruption.

"Yeah, I heard about it," Ben said, "but I had to go down below Middleon and get the contractor back on a tract of land. Tenant flooded them out and promised to shoot the first man who got back on his land. It was one of old Hank's clients, and he either missed a tenant or died before he got him to sign. It seemed like it was more important to get that mess straightened out."

"You're probably right," Wiley thought the matter over and agreed. "Did you say the construction crew got flooded out? It hasn't rained in six weeks. How did they get flooded out?"

"Jim Golden is tenant on the Montgomery tract, and he claims he wasn't contacted before they started building across his cotton field. I talked to Montgomery and he says that Jim's telling a damn lie. Jim opened the sluice on his water storage and flooded the Moore crew a little after dinner on Friday. It turned into one hell of a mess. Leroy Moon, the crew pusher, says that water came in like a tidal wave. The whole damn crew piled in one pickup and made it to high ground, but all their other equipment wound up in a mud hole. Everybody was mad as a wet hen when I got down there Sunday morning."

"Are they back at work?" Wiley asked.

"Not yet," Ben said, "but they can get back on the land by Tuesday. That ground soaks up the water pretty quick. Leroy moved his crew two tracts south and says they'll go back as soon as the ground's dry enough. Nobody was real happy when I left, but I don't think there'll be any bloodshed."

"You did right," Wiley admitted. "but you should have called in about the meeting."

"I know," Ben said, "and I meant to, but it slipped my mind. I'm here now—am I too late for some of the meeting? I don't have to hit the road until tomorrow."

"Do you even know what the meeting is about?"

"Yeah, Brad told me that we're getting five new land buyers."

"Exactly," Wiley said. "I'd hoped you could be here for the whole meeting, since we're going to be looking to you to monitor them until they get their feet on the ground. They're good men and they're being transferred to engineering from other departments. None of them have ever negotiated for right of way though."

"I'll do what I can, " Ben replied warily, "but I'll tell you right now that right of way buying must be learned, but I don't think it can be taught."

"Weren't you taught?"

"Nope, they gave me a handful of easements, a car and a check book and told me they needed land to build on—and no excuses."

"Who's they?"

"Vernon Marmaduke and Dill Scratch, they'd never bought any right of way either, so they couldn't be of any help," Ben said.

"Didn't Brown and Gankle help you when you were breaking in?" Brad asked.

"In a way," Ben smiled, "they culled all the potential condemnations out on the 138KV line from Big River to Sutter and gave them to me. It was my option as to whether I'd sink or swim. That's the way they were broke in too."

"Well," Wiley said," we're on coffee break. What I want you to do is to go down there and wrap up the proceedings. We've already been over the forms and some of the details of our right of way buying practices." Wiley glanced at his watch. "There's two hours left in the day and you can tell them more in an hour than I could tell them in a week."

"When are they actually going on the payroll as land buyers?"

"Tomorrow—if they accept, and I expect they all will. Either they become right of way buyers or wind up as meter readers. We need them in the field within two weeks. We've got three hundred miles of right of way to buy and only six months to get it. Any reason why that can't happen?"

"If we're lucky and if two or three of your new agents work out I figure it can be done," Ben replied. "Judging on that length, there shouldn't be over five or six hundred tracts in the whole taking. Is the abstracting and aerial photography done?"

"Five hundred and thirty five tracts, according to Bill Lowery, he's already at work on the legal descriptions and the easements won't take all that long once the metes and bounds are calculated," Brad said. "We're going to be able to wind up the preparation as soon as a ground survey is done. Naturally, we need survey permission first. That's where you come in Ben. You and your troops."

"Why don't you get on down to the conference room and introduce yourself to our new agents. You can work out the details and form a plan of action. I'll appreciate your cooperation in this Ben. And I know you can do it!" Wiley said. "I've got things to take care of in my office, but I'll be checking with you later Brad," Wiley left the room and was whistling a little tune as he exited past Ruby Jean's desk. She smiled her sweetest smile and wished Mr. Kyle a pleasant week. She wished Ben a good day as he followed in his wake.

"Hang in there Ruby," Ben said. "Be good."

"You know I will. Don't forget to call in and keep me posted on your location."

"Trust me."

chapter XIV

J. J. was shuffling through his documents when Ben entered the room. J.J. had assumed that Wiley Kiel would be returning and he had been listing his questions while the others were drinking coffee. He had a tough time keeping his mind from wondering what they might hear about him losing his position in the break room. It would be just like that Roberta to be broadcasting the news of the treatment he'd gotten. He'd always suspected that she resented his authority, and if he could do it all over again he would not report her performance as "Satisfactory".

Not even Sid could help him now, and that's exactly what he'd told J. J. "Just make the best of it," he'd said, "and don't let me down, land buying should be a snap for you. You've always had a way with people, and that's half the requirement. You may be pleasantly surprised at the possibilities that come with your new assignment." Sid's words cheered J. J. a little, but he needed a lot of cheering. He did not get much from Nancy.

"I knew it was too good to last," had been her observation. "Without Daddy, you may wind up without a job!"

"How're you doing J. J.?" Ben greeted him. "I haven't seen you in a good while. Wiley Kiel tells me that you're thinking about going into the land buying business."

"Looks like," J. J. stood and shook hands. "Mr. Kiel says he's in a bind for negotiators, and I've always wanted to try my hand at it. A man can get tired of the same old routine, day in and day out. Being the Employee Benefits Co-Ordinator can be stressful and the responsibilities are great. You know, I had forgotten that you are an agent. Don't see you very often, and even on those rare occasions we don't ever seem to have time to visit."

"Ain't that the truth," Ben said. "I hardly ever get to your place. We've had so much going on I don't even see my wife and kid over two or three times a month. When I'm on the road I spend a good deal of time in coffee shops, but I miss the coffee you and Roberta brew up." Ben sat down and propped his muddy boots on the table corner. When he saw that the mud was not completely dry he removed them and found a wastebasket and moved it before his chair. He took his knife from his pocket and set about the task of scraping what he could from his feet. He was still at it when the other four men trooped back into the room and sat down.

"I had a kind of dirty job this weekend," Ben said." "I was supposed to be here for this meeting, but I'm running late. I got here as soon as I could. Ran into Wiley Kiel up in Brad Hare's office and he told me to get down here and wrap this up. You all most likely have homes to go to so we'll try and get it done."

"Who are you?" Kent asked.

"Ben Drill".

"How long have you been on the job?" Hal asked. "I don't think I've ever seen you before."

"I've got a desk down the hall," Ben said, "but I don't spend much time around the office. I don't know any of you men either, but I've been on the payroll for thirty-two years. Since I was discharged from the Army. If you guys take this job, we'll probably see a lot of each other—but not here."

"Will Mr. Kiel be back?" J. B. asked.

"No" Ben said. "He's turned the last rites over to me. He asked me to tell you what right of way buying is like. I'm not a speaker and I'm not sure I can tell you much, but I'll give it my best shot. Probably, one way is to tell you what I did last week. I'll probably ramble, but like I said, I'm no orator. I'll be working with you if you decide to come into engineering and we'll iron out the details as we go along."

Ben then told the group of the line he was negotiating in West Texas, the construction underway in High Bank and toward Whitlow. He was getting primed to tell them of the rapid tempo, major undertaking that would begin fifty miles west of Metroplex and extend to the Petroplex cities of Midway and Vast Plain, when he noticed that it was nearing 4 P.M. and the five men were weary of listening.

"Fellers, I'll tell you what—I'm gonna cut this short and get us all out of here. If ya'll decide to get into the land buying business we'll have plenty of time to get acquainted once you're on the job. Ya'll are used to these office doings, but I ain't much of a hand to hang around here— I've got irons in the fire and need to hit the road.

"They'll furnish you a company car, an expense account, a telephone credit card, and a check book. They'll qualify you as a Notary, and pay the annual fee. You will be your own boss, on a straight salary and work whatever hours it takes to get the job done. That can, and probably will include nights and weekends when the ox is in the ditch, and the construction crew is nipping at your butt. It's a pressure job sometimes, which I personally enjoy. You won't sleep with your own wife on a regular basis, but you'll get used to that too.

"Kiel recommends 'copious notes' of your contacts and an accurate record of the negotiation—just in case we wind up in condemnation court. TLC frowns on going to court, but it happens sometimes. So, try not to say "Eminent Domain' or 'Condemnation' to a land owner except as a last resort. You're not about to make any friends by taking land through condemnation proceedings.

"I wouldn't trade my job for Vernon Marmaduke's—It's a hell of a game and it ain't boring. You may or may not feel the same way, but if you're willing to give it a try it won't take long for you to figure out if it's what you want to do.

"I've got to be in Vast Plain at eight o'clock tomorrow morning, and I figure you guys have some thinking to do and maybe a wife to talk to, so I'm gonna quit right here. I haven't told you much, I know, but you'll be around Brad Hare and the office bunch down in Engineering the rest of the week getting tooled up for life on the front line.

"I'm supposed to be in Chalk Draw next Monday morning—a week from today, and you will either be there ready to go to work, or not there at all. If you show up we'll get together and work out our crusade for three or four hundred miles of right of way." Ben paused and resumed the scraping of mud from his boots.

"How long did you say you've been a right of way buyer?" Kent asked.

"Around thirty two years", Ben said. "Sometimes it seems like all my life."

"And you really like it?"

"I don't really like to work at all, if that's what you're asking. But I'd a helluva lot rather buy land as push a pencil or read meters."

"I have a number of questions," J. J. began to leaf through his steno notebook. "First of all..."

"It's four thirty and I'm out of here," Ben closed his knife and put it into his pocket. "Just hang onto your questions and we'll get around to them next week. Or, corner Brad Hare tomorrow. He ain't bought any right of way but he's been Chief Construction Engineer for a long time, and he can most likely tell you anything you want to know."

"It was my pleasure to meet you, and I'm looking forward to working with you but I've got to hit the road." Ben rose and walked out the door.

"What do you all think?" Bob asked. They packaged their exhibits and papers prepatory to leaving.

"Hot damn!" Hal said. "I like the car, the expense account and not having some supervisor looking over my shoulder eight hours a day. I'm ready to sign on."

"I can't see that we've got any option," Kent observed. "It's either take this job or not have one. I kinda think I'll like it."

"I hope my wife will let me try it," Bill said. "She don't much like for me to be away from home at night, but life's been hell since I lost my manager's job. I plan on being in Chalk Draw next Monday!"

"I guess I will too," J. J. said as he put all his papers back into the manila envelope, "but I still have a lot of questions for somebody to answer."

Chapter XV

Bill Clemons finally managed to negotiate an escape and leave the bustling Metro Plex traffic behind him as he returned to his home in Ringer. Florence heard his car door open and close and she met him at the entryway.

"How did things go?" she asked. "Do we still have a job?"

"Yes we do," Bill said, "and it may be a better deal than we've ever had! It could be better than my local manager job. Anything is better than that flunky job I've had since they closed the office," he added.

As Florence busied with grilled cheese sandwich preparation Bill sat with his "Grandpa" cup of steaming coffee and described the events of his day.

Of major importance, of course, was having a company car again. He had missed that company car almost as much as his Local Manager designation. He told Florence of the other perks, having his own company check book, calling cards and an expense account. His work area was to be system wide and the freedom to do his work was unprecedented. Of course, he had superiors, but they would put their trust in him and allow him to do his work without interference. Lastly, he confessed that he might be on the job seven days a week at times, and away from the house for extended periods of time.

"I'll be on the road," Bill said. "Wherever the company needs land will be my work area. That's the only part I'm not sure I like."

"We'll manage," Florence said, and her lack of hysteria was a pleasant surprise to Bill. "I'll worry about you getting lost, and I want your word that you'll stay out of the dance halls."

"You can count on that," Bill said. "Most of the time I'll be home on weekends and the way we have to move around I doubt I'll even think about dancing. I'll do that with you when I get home."

"How many land buyers are there?" Florence asked," and do you know any of them?"

"There's only one now," Bill said, "but the company plans to put me and four others in the field for training. TLC has a big expansion planned and Ben, the one they've got now, can't do the land buying by himself."

"Only one?" Florence said.

Bill told of the abrupt decimation of TLC's acquisition team, and admitted that he did not know any of the other chosen replacements. He added that he had never heard of Ben Drill.

"He's sort of different," was the way Bill put it. "He's in his mid fifties. He's tall and skinny and don't wear a suit or tie. And, his boots were muddy. None of the other men knew much about him, but he's been working for the company for more than thirty years. He'll meet with us a week from Monday at Chalk Draw and help us get started on a big project. This week we'll be around the Engineering office getting familiar with the paper work and meeting everyone. I'm scared, but I think I can do the job and I know it can't be as bad as what I've put up with since they closed my office."

The phone rang as Florence set his sandwich on the table. She answered and handed the receiver to Bill.

"Hey J. B., this is Dusty. How'd you come out over in the big city?"

"O.K.. I think I'm going to like my new job. Only bad thing is, I'll miss our golf games."

"Yeah," Dusty said. "I enjoyed it while it lasted, but I've already got me a new partner, so the game will go on."

"Who will you be playing with?"

"John Darby. Your old boss. He volunteered for the job."

Bob Barrick, Harold Ackers and Kent Fields appeared in unison at Marv Freeman's office and announced that they had made the decision to accept transfer from Customer Service to the Engineering Department.

Marv wished them luck and assured them that he would be behind them "all the way". They cleaned their personal belongings from their workstations and left with their cardboard boxes of take-outs. They left more in the wastebaskets than they carried home.

Kent told Lilly approximately the same story as Bill told Florence and Harold filed a similar story with his wife Velma. Bob Barrick did not have a wife to report to, since he was a drummer in a C&W Band, "The Shysters" but he passed his information along to them.

"Maybe you can get us some gigs in some of those towns you'll be working in. You'll still be our main drummer when you're home on weekends, but we'll come to where you are if you find us a deal where we can put cash in our pockets," Sam, the band leader said.

"You got a deal," Bob said, "I figure I'll have time to hustle us some dates while I'm on the road. Maybe even hustle me some dates where I don't need backup."

J. J. made a glowing presentation to Nancy. As far as he could tell, he'd found a bird nest on the ground, and his new and possible importance was a pleasant thing for him to think about.

"Nancy," he said, "I believe that I can rise to the top in the land acquisition department. I met the ace agent in the department and I can drop him like an Otis elevator."

"What's his name?"

"Ben something, and from his looks he's about used up. I think I'll call Sid."

"Daddy called and said that he didn't want to hear any more about your transfer. He said that he don't even like to think about TLC. He said they can all go to hell as far as he's concerned!"

J. J. went to his clothes closet. He had a pair of cowboy boots in there somewhere and he meant to find them. He'd not worn them as Employee Benefits Supervisor, but it would be nice to put them back on and add two inches to his height. Tomorrow, he meant to buy a supply of designer jeans.

"And Sid," he muttered, "you can go to hell for all I care!"

Chapter XVI

A week had come and gone since Ben had been out to the Kelly Ranch and he figured the time was right for a second trip. If Goose hadn't died of snakebites Ben needed to make a second run at him and get negotiations another notch along.

Some days Ben felt like he was on top of his game, and there was no better place to check out the accuracy of his feeling than a tete-a-tete with Goose. Construction of Voltaire Sulphur Substation and its 345 KV umbilical cord was scheduled to begin July 1, and that date was but a little more than a month away. The brain trust had already begun to get antsy and every time he called in, some engineer or the other was looking for him.

He knew the regular coffee and lunchtime for the callers, and thoughtfully returned their calls when they were away from their desks. Naturally, he feigned disappointment at missing connections, and always assured their secretaries or assistants that he'd be calling back when he had the chance. Then, he didn't call back.

Goose was standing in his front yard as Ben stopped his car and rolled his window down. Goose glanced at the car, recognized Ben and invited him to get out. Moose did not appear, so Ben alit and walked across the yard.

Goose stood over a box terrapin and held a straightened coat hanger in his hand. Ben noted that both his hands had returned to just about normal size. A strip of duct tape covered the bitten area, but Goose seemed to be in fine shape and was smiling as Ben walked up.

"Your hands look good as new," Ben said, "that coal oil did the trick."

"Always does," Goose said. "I'm ready to go another round with a rattlesnake or two."

"What are you doing with that box turtle?" Ben asked, and his curiosity was genuine.

"I'm training him for the turtle race," Goose said. "It comes off next month and I aim to win me another blue ribbon."

"Turtle race? I've never heard of a turtle race. Where do they have it, and how can you make a turtle race?"

"It's helt over at Brisco every July," Goose said. "I've won it for the last nine years! When I win this year the Chevy dealer over at Cielo Vista will have to give me a brand new pickup. I've only been getting a thousand dollars a year, and a blue ribbon, in the past, but when I pull off win number ten I get a new pickup. I'll show it to you when you're out this way."

"Can you make him go?" Ben asked. "He's got his head and all his running gear pulled into his shell and it don't look like he'll come out until it thunders. I've always heard that's the only time you can count on them to get moving."

" He'll take off when I want him to," Goose smiled. "I've got him trained and ready to go! I believe he's faster than the one I had last year, and that slow pole won by five minutes. He crossed the line before some the other entries moved a peg."

"Let's see you make him go," Ben said, "I don't doubt your word, but I'd sure like to see him move out."

"Sure," Goose smiled and tapped the turtle shell with his coat hanger. Head and legs appeared as if by magic and the turtle moved ahead as fast as his stubby legs could carry him. He went about six feet and retracted his legs and head. Goose tapped him again and the terrapin re-activated and in the twinkle of an eye he was back to full speed.

"Well I'll be damned!" Ben said in wonder. "That beats anything I've ever seen. How in the world do you train a racing turtle? And where did you learn how?"

"I learnt myself," Goose said proudly, "but my training method is secret. If it got out everybody in the whole world would have a racing turtle, so I keep it to myself. That little bugger is gonna win me a new pickup truck!"

"I'd bet money on him," Ben admitted.

"Let's us go in the house where it's cool," Goose said as he picked up his turtle. He held it at arm's length so that the stream of urine would not hit his pants or boots, and deposited it in a number three washtub beneath the lip of the high porch deck. Goose wiped his hand on his shirtfront and preceded Ben into the front room, and both climbed into a glistening barber chair. Goose tilted his back and closed his eyes in ecstasy.

"Fantastic seating," Ben said. "You lead a mighty interesting life Mr. Kelly. You're the only man I know with two barber chairs and a racing turtle. By the way, what's the turtle's name?"

"Rocket," Goose smiled. "He's going to win me a brand new truck for sure! This will be the first time anybody ever won ten years in a row. Old Sam Gore, who owns that Chevy Dealership is going to scream like a wounded panther, since I ain't never bought a pickup from him. I go to Vast Plain and buy me a Ford when I need one. You going to be in this country next month? I'd like you to come out and see the race."

"I'd like to see it," Ben admitted. "If I'm not all tied up I'll be there."

"Good," Goose said. "You can drive me over in your car so I'll be able to get my pickup home. I'd be much obliged."

"My bosses are getting worried and putting pressure on me to get the right of way bought so we can get our line built," Ben said. "If I could know that you and me are going to trade I think I might manage to get a day off and go to that race. But, no matter what, you've got my word—if I can manage it I'll haul you and Rocket over there and help get your new rig back home."

"Let's see if we can make a trade right now then" Goose said. "Tell me where you want to build and how much the Light Company will pay."

"Welsir," Ben said, "our survey line is a quarter mile north and parallel to the railroad across your fifteen miles of land. Then it goes straight on west across five miles of the Cruickshank Jones Ranch. From there it continues west on the Simon Pleska place for two miles and then turns north toward Voltaire County. I've already talked to Mr. Jones and Mr. Pleska and they told me that if you agree to sell us an easement they will too, at the price you agree to. According to my information all three of you use the same attorney."

"Yeah, we all use Christopher Finn. He makes sure we get a fair shake on land deals. Tell me about that damn electric line again. Did you say it was on steel posts?"

"Four legged towers actually. We didn't want to put any more creosoted posts across your place. That cresote kills the vegetation. Steel don't affect the grass. Best of all, it only takes five of them to cross a mile—they stand better than a thousand feet apart on flat ground.

"We put up a good steel gate in every cross fence and buy you however many locks you need for the gates on your place. Your lock is in series with ours. We don't give our key to anyone and you'll be the only one with a key to your locks. You and the company can both use those gates, but we'll not be on your land again unless an act of God takes our line down—and that is not likely with four legged towers. But, if we did have to come out on a stormy night and put a downed line back up we'll pay you for the damages. I'll be the one who shows up to settle the damage claim and I guarantee you—they don't pay me enough salary to lie, or try and cheat a man!"

"I checked you out the last time you built on me," Goose said. "You treated me square and the neighbors have the same opinion. Your company gets by with paying less money than the oil companies, but you don't cause us near the headaches. Now, what will you pay?"

"The right of way is a hundred and fifty feet wide," Ben said," or approximately eighteen acres to the mile. We believe a fair compensation for this crossing is twenty five hundred dollars to the mile. If you figure it by the tower it's five hundred for each tower. Or, by the acre it figures to approximately a hundred and forty dollars. The land is still yours and if you ever sell the place that eighteen acres is sold right along with the rest."

"That ain't enough money," Goose said without emotion. "We get more than that for a mile of two inch surface pipe line from the oil companies. We sell them right of way by the rod and they pay three thousand for a mile of temporary line. They scream rape, but they pay off to stay out of the courthouse. Chris Finn has made believers out of them, and he'd have a stroke if I took you up on your offer."

Ben asked permission to smoke a cigarette and Goose told him it would be all right. "I don't smoke, but they don't bother me when somebody else does," was the way he put it. Goose inspected his duct taped hands and Ben smoked in silence, dumping the ash into his shirt pocket. Neither spoke as he finished his smoke, went outside, field stripped the butt and stepped on the burning end. He wadded the paper skin into a pill and put it in his pocket. He doubted Goose would notice a Sherman Tank discarded in that yard, but his hitch in the Army had ingrained habits that were observed unconsciously. He always fieldstripped his cigarettes, and that task was simple due to the fact that he smoked filter free cigarettes. Ben was convinced that the filters were what caused cancer. He went back inside and climbed back into his barber chair.

"What would it take to trade with you Mr. Kelly?" Ben asked. "TLC is an investor owned utility company and frugality is our nature, but we try to be reasonable and avoid court houses. We, of course, have legal rights, but moral rights are a heap more important. We have the right of eminent domain, but we haven't gained many friends using it."

"I believe a thousand dollars a stand would be about right," Goose said." I know that's double what you offered, but five thousand dollars a mile ain't all that much money anymore."

"I'd be on unemployment tomorrow if I agreed to that kind of money," Ben said as he looked glumly at the screen door. "Is there any wiggle room between our figures that I could take to 'Daddy' for consideration? Our Appraisal Department furnishes me with their opinion of a fair price, but I'm not against taking a counter offer to the throne room. But I guarantee you they won't even consider a thousand dollars a structure."

"Tell you what," Goose said after a lengthy silence. "You get me seven hundred and fifty dollars a stand and I'll get you twenty one miles of your right of way tomorrow!"

"Twenty two miles," Ben corrected.

"Twenty one," said Goose. "I forgot to tell you that I let Miss Frances Holiman have a section four miles from my east line. She's the one I got these barber chairs from. I told her about your line. It crosses her section too. But," Goose smiled, "I can get that mile for you. She'll listen to what I advise her to do. You've got to go and meet Miss Frances. She's one of a kind."

"I thought I saw a building out there," Ben said. "I figured it was an oil company shed or something you'd put up. What does Miss Frances do?"

"You'll have to go and see for yourself Ben," Goose said. "You wouldn't believe me if I told you! But I guarantee you that she's one of a kind!"

"Welsir," Ben said, "I 've got your word that we can trade at seven hundred and fifty dollars a structure. You've got my word that I'm going to do my dead level best to get the company to go along. I've got to get back over to Vast Plain now and take care of some things, but I'll talk to my boss today, tonight, or this weekend at his home if necessary, and I'll be back here by the middle of the morning next Tuesday." Ben and Goose shook hands on the deal, with Ben being extra careful of Goose's bandaged hand. They walked across the yard to Ben's car.

"If I can pull this off," Ben said, "There's one thing I want out of the deal."

"What's that," Goose was startled.

"I want to know how you trained that turtle to run."

Goose smiled, turned and went back toward the porch. He reached in the tub and put Rocket on the ground. Then he retrieved his coat hanger and resumed his training. One tap put Rocket at top speed.

Things had gone to suit Ben, so he decided to run over to the Holiman place and meet with Goose's new neighbor. He was curious to learn what qualified her as "one of a kind".

chapter XVII

Watching his odometer, Ben drove due north for a half-mile after he left the Interstate and crossed the railroad, so he calculated that the Frances Holiman residence was located near the center of her square mile of territory. He was unable to imagine how she had managed to buy any part of the Kelly Ranch. Goose had told him that she was "one of a kind" and Ben was anxious to see for himself what manner of woman could beguile Goose Kelly into deeding away even a square foot of land.

As Ben topped a gentle rise he saw the red brick house nestled in a grove of mesquite and desert willow. The trees were not tall enough to shade the roof, but with time and water the site could develop into an oasis in the sea of sand, caliche and Russian thistle wilds.

A wooden tined windmill stood near the house and a huge cypress storage tank gave testimony, by its dark coloration, to the availability of water. Water is a plentiful resource beneath most of the vast flats of the dried up Permian Sea, but that abundance provides little comfort to those who depend on it for drinking purposes. Gyp water is hard enough to support a driven nail, and when that water evaporates it leaves a residue not unlike sheet rock. It will however, sustain life and Ben saw immediate evidence of that truth.

As he proceeded slowly toward the house he saw burros, goats, rangy long horn cattle and all manner of livestock. Swimming in the half-acre earthen tank were ducks, geese and bronze turkey flocks wandered the shinnery looking for something to eat. He stopped near a Ford Van with four flat tires and an ancient Dodge pickup truck, which suffered the same affliction. Flocks of mixed variety chickens, guineas and scores of cats came on the run to see who had arrived and perhaps mooch a bite of food. Ben was traveling light on any manner of foodstuff for them, so he sat immobile in his Tempo and waited hopefully for the appearance of a human being.

His patience paid off. The most shabby specimen of humanity he'd beheld in a good while tentatively appeared from the back of the house. It was impossible to tell whether it was a man or a woman, but whichever it was had on enough layers of clothing to survive an Alaskan winter. In the hand of that person was a pitchfork and the figure stood quietly and awaited Ben's next move. Not a word was spoken as a huge yellow dog materialized to the rear of the pitchfork bearer and stood attentively, waiting for orders.

"Howdy," Ben spoke up loudly enough to be heard, "Is Miz Holiman around?" Ben was almost sure he was speaking to a hired hand, or maybe even Mr. Holiman. He couldn't remember whether Goose had told him if there was a Mr. Holiman.

"Who are you, and what do you want?" The person and dog moved forward to a better hearing range, but still thirty feet from Ben's car.

"My name is Ben Drill. Mr. Kelly told me that I needed to come by and meet Miz Holiman. Is she in the house, and would she have time to speak with me on a matter of business?"

"Don't get out. I'll come closer to your car. I've got my dog with me, so don't make any sudden moves. He's a biting dog, and he'll bite whatever or whoever I tell him to." By the time the figure came within ten feet, Ben decided that it might be a woman, but he was unsure and he selected his words with care as the distance between them diminished. The dog stayed just to the rear and the pitch fork was still prominent in the right hand.

"Miz Holiman?" Ben slurred his "Mrs." so that it would require canine caliber hearing to know whether he'd said Mr. or Mrs.

"Of course I'm Frances Holiman" the woman said. "Who else could I be?"

"Well" Ben said, "you looked so young I thought maybe you were a daughter. Mr. Kelly didn't tell me whether or not you have children."

"I have many children," she stared fixedly and unblinking at Ben. "These creatures you see are my children. The Lord called me to care for his helpless creations in this wicked and uncaring land and time!" She looked proudly around at her teeming zoo.

"Well, I'd say the Lord made a wise decision when he called you," Ben said, "from what I've seen you've got contented herds and flocks and they all seem to be doing well. Do you sell them?"

"I should say not!" she stated emphatically. "If I sold them to the wrong person harm could come to them. Mr. Drill, there are people who slay and consume both animal and fowl, but I'm sure you are aware of that fact. No harm will ever come to my children for so long as I have breath in my body." She emphasized her statement by punching doodlebug holes in the sand with the fork handle.

"Admirable," Ben said. "The world needs more people like you Mrs. Holiman. Mr. Kelly told me that before I came over here."

"You can get out and tell me your business now, but I'm Miss Holiman. My sweetheart died on Normandy Beach in the War. At least, that's what they told me. I know better, but you wouldn't care about that matter!"

Ben got out and followed Miss Holiman and the dog to the best shade and found a seat on a bleached out round of high line pole. Miss Holiman and the dog sat on a full width car seat supported by four cinder blocks. A cast iron wash pot rested upside down between the two seating locations.

Ben explained the necessity for building an electric transmission line across Miss Holiman's acreage, and she listened patiently and without interruption until he completed his abridged presentation.

"Mr. Kelly told me that you'd be by," she admitted, "and he also told me that you can be trusted. He did not tell me how much money you will pay—he said that he would take care of all that. When you work out the details with Mr. Kelly he will tell me and I will sign your papers, as long as I do not have to go to town and appear before a notary. I don't go to town."

"I'm a notary," Ben said, "and I can write your check and hand it to you." He looked down at the cast iron wash pot and noticed a small black paw extend out from under the rim. It was a kitten's paw and it raked the hardpan surface of the ground in a futile effort to dig out. The clawed groove was barely ample to allow air into the cast iron dome.

"There's a kitten under that wash pot," Ben reported. "He's going to bake when the sun's at twelve o'clock. Do you want me to lift the side and let him out?"

"Of course not! That's Samantha and she's atoning for her sin. She killed little Charlie and ate him! He'd not been out of the egg a week when she fell upon him and committed her murderous act. She is eligible for release tomorrow." A tear coursed down Miss Holiman's weathered cheek as she recalled the gory end to Charlie's short life.

"Samantha might not make it until tomorrow" Ben said. "She seems to be clawing mighty weak."

"She's got a bowl of water and a crust of bread," Miss Holiman said. "She'll live, but you can rest assured that when I turn her out tomorrow she won't be tempted to kill any more innocent chicks!"

"I'll bet you're right," Ben admitted. "I guess I'll get along and do my job. I enjoyed the visit and I'll see you again when Mr. Kelly and I get everthing worked out. It should be in the next week or two." Ben walked to his car, got in and looked back as Miss Holiman ascended a slanted board and vanished into the house through a window. He backed out carefully and made for the Interstate at a reduced rate of speed. All the various life forms moving around the Holiman acreage were ceded the right of way. Ben could not help but imagine spending a couple of days in a dark cast iron cell with only bread and water, as punishment for flattening a chicken.

"Son of a Bitch!" he said as he turned his radio on.

Chapter XVIII

Ben wheeled into a Quick Sax Grocery parking lot and jockeyed into a position that allowed him in car access to a pay phone. He dialed the operator, gave her his card number and the number for Brad Hare. Of course Ruby answered the phone.

"Need to talk to Brad," Ben said. "And oh yeah, good morning to you and all the wage slaves at the corporate throne room."

"I wish I was with you darling," Ruby whispered. "I think about you all the time." Ben rolled his side glass down and the roar and clatter of traffic increased the difficulty of subdued telephone conversation.

"It's kinda hard to understand you over this loud traffic," Ben said, "so I've got to make this short. Is Brad in his office?"

"He's on another line," Ruby said. "But I'll talk to you until he gets off."

"O.K.," Ben said, "but you'll have to talk loud. I'm at an outside booth and there's a lot of traffic. So be careful what you talk about. Everyone in the office will be able to hear you."

"Yes," she replied, "I understand. Where are you?"

"About halfway between Minotaur and Flat Land. I'm on my way back east, so I'm not checked in at any motel yet, and I can't say yet where I'll spend the night. Are those five draftee negotiators driving everybody crazy with their questions?"

"Yes they are. Especially Mr. Tolliver. Brad keeps his door closed and I have orders not to let him go in. They're working at getting ready for next week. I guess they're kind of scared about having a different job, and wonder if they'll be able to do it."

"Hell!" Ben said. "If I can do this job a chimpanzee can be trained to do it in two weeks."

"I doubt that—just a moment—Brad's off the phone. Bye, bye, and you be sure and let me know how I can get hold of you, do you understand?" Ben understood and winced.

"Brad Hare," Brad came on line. "How can I help you?"

"Give me a raise," Ben said as he rolled his window up so that he could hear and be heard.

"I've been trying to get one for myself Ben. If I manage it I'll go to work and try to get you one too. What do you really need?"

"Nothing," Ben said. "You can put the survey crew to work on the route for the line to Voltaire County Sulphur. We've got the right of way for the whole shebang."

"Are the easements in your hands?" Brad asked.

"No, I've got to have old Herb rewrite the Kelly taking. There's a new, one section owner on an island in the ranch. Herb needs to call the abstract company today and get the information. Then I want him to mail all four instruments to Christopher Finn's office over in Merrit. The land owners will go by and sign, and we'll wrap up the whole thing."

"Then, you've only got their word—is that what you're telling me?" Brad was always cautious when Ben made one of his "hand shake" deals.

"That's true," Ben said, "but Pete Kelly's word is as good as a signed easement. Will you pass the information on to Herb about the new owner? Her name is Frances Holiman, and I figure she's been on the land for a couple of years, but he can get the accurate scoop from the abstract company. He can get it with a call easier than I can go by there and dig it out."

"Yeah, I'll get Herb to handle it—but are you sure we can trust those owners to execute the easements. Finn hates us and nobody knows it better than you. I sure as hell don't trust that bastard. He'd rob a blind man!"

"He may not like us," Ben said, "but he likes the retainer he gets from Goose Kelly every month."

"Okay, if you say so. We'll send the survey crew over in the next couple of days and stake the tower locations, but I'm not going to authorize the construction crew to go to work until those easements are signed, sealed and recorded in the court house records!"

"Fair enough—it'll be done next week," Ben assured Brad. "How are your new agents doing? Are they girding their loins for battle?"

"Seem to be. We've got cars for them and they're all set to come out to Chalk Draw next week – or wherever you told them to. I'm ready to get them out of here—especially that Tolliver. He'd drive a sane man crazy in three days with all his damn questions. I think land owners might sign his easements just to get rid of him," Brad said.

"It don't work that way," Ben smiled. "They'll just run him off the place when their ears get to ringing. All five of them might make good agents once they get weaned of hanging around an office."

"I hope you're right," Brad said. "The next couple of years are going to be a pair to draw to. More projects than we've had on the drawing board since back in the fifties. And by the way, where are you staying this week?"

"I haven't lit yet," Ben admitted. "I was about halfway figuring on going up toward High Bank, I haven't been up there in two or three weeks."

"They must be doing alright," Brad said. "We've not heard anything to the contrary—no news is good news. There's a situation over at Dry Lake that you need to see about. I was just on the phone with Roy Glenn and he's got a problem with a couple of land owners over in his division."

"What kind of problem is that?"

"Something about the 69KV line to Westhaven. They're working maintenance on it and two landowners shut the work down and ran his agent off. He asked for help in getting things smoothed out."

"What are the land owner's names?"

"I didn't write them down," Brad confessed, "but since Dry Lake is right on your way you need to stop by and see what you can do to stop Roy's ulcers from growing any bigger. You know how he over-reacts to trouble."

"Tell Ruby Jean that I'll be at the Homefolk Inn in Dry Lake," Ben said, "if they've got a room. If they don't, I'll be somewhere else and I'll be back in touch tomorrow."

"I'll do it. Good luck! Roy Glenn will appreciate the help."

"Bullshit!" Ben said. "Roy Glenn don't appreciate anything. I'll be at his office at eight in the morning, but I'm not going to call and tell him I'm coming. His ulcers can gnaw on him all night as far as I'm concerned." Ben rolled down his glass, recradled the telephone, and drove to Polly's Diner for coffee and breakfast. "That's one damn phone call I ought not to have made," he muttered to himself. "It'll be awhile before I make that mistake again!"

Chapter XIX

Roy Glenn was a product of Texas A&M University and a typical Aggie in every sense of the word. His hubcap dimension graduation ring was displayed prominently and his bearing was ramrod ROTC. He'd only been in the employment of TLC for five years but his belief in organization and discipline was zealous. He had achieved the title and position of Division Engineer of Dry Lake Division in that short span of years. That progress was a delight to him and a hellish experience for many of his employees. Especially, James Lemond who served as Division Right of Way Representative.

James had lost his company pickup within a week after Roy's arrival and now had to borrow a vehicle, when he could establish a legitimate need. Emergencies were a rare commodity in the sleepy Dry Lake Division and the loss of his transportation had imposed limits on James' freedom to escape the office and frequent the coffee shops. "Emasculated" was the way James described his condition.

Ben arrived at seven thirty and James sat at one of the masonite tables, nursing a styrofoam cup of coffee and puffing a Kool. Ben drew a cup and sat down across from him. The two men had known each other for several years and James nodded as Ben lit a smoke.

"How're things going?" Ben asked, but it was evident that James was not all that glad to see him, so he continued, "I'm not here by choice James. I've got a boss and he told me to come by. He's an Aggie too and I couldn't come up with a reason why I couldn't make it."

"I know," James said. "You're the only one left aren't you? I hear that Brown died and old Gankle retired."

"That's a fact," Ben admitted. "Hank checked into the hospital, but they carried him out. It was a heart attack or something. Gankle was way past retirement age, and he had to go to satisfy company policy. Tim

Burkeen is in a nursing home as a result of a head-on car wreck while he was on vacation. All of a sudden I'm the only one left."

"Well," James said, "I don't envy you your job—being on the road all the time—I like sleeping in my own bed at night, but some days I'm tempted to put in for a transfer. Working conditions can be a bitch around here. Are they looking for agents down at the main office?"

"Damn if I know," Ben said. "They don't tell me anything and I don't ask. I'll be eligible for retirement next year, and that's exactly what I'm going to do. A hotshot down in our insurance department told me that the retirees at sixty-five draw an average of eighteen checks. I plan to add ten years to that year and a half if I can stay out of a car wreck until January."

Roy Glenn arrived at five minutes before eight and he found James and Ben drinking their coffee. He eyed them suspiciously as he filled his cup and walked over.

"Are you two plotting against me?" he asked. He tried to make his question sound like humor, but it did not come across that way to James, who blushed guiltily.

"We're plotting the overthrow of the whole damn world," Ben said. "It ain't going to suit us and we're thinking about rebellion!" He, stood and shook Roy's hand. "Brad asked me to drop by for some reason—so here I am."

"I need to talk to both of you," Roy said. "Why don't we go into my office?" They rose and James followed closely as Ben poured a warm up.

"The Bingham boys bowed up yesterday and ran my crew off their farm," Roy began as he seated himself behind his desk, "and a brother-in-law of theirs, Dilbert Sweat, came out of the woodwork and he's raising hell down at the east end of the line. He says that we're not coming on his place either.

"The company bought easements from their daddies back in the thirties and we have authority to enter both places for maintenance and reconstruction. Mr. Lemond, will you get your copy of those instruments and give them to Mr. Drill?"

"Yes sir, Mr. Glenn," James arose and left the office. He closed the door behind him.

"Ben," Roy said, "I guess Brad told you that we've got to get back on these tracts damn quick. I sent a boy to do a man's work when I sent James Lemond. I don't know what he did wrong, but I know they ran his ass off and he came back here with his tail between his legs. He wanted me to get the Sheriff to go back out there with him and enforce our lawful rights. He's the sorriest right of way agent in the whole company and that's exactly what I told him! I called Brad and asked for you. He says you can handle this situation and I'll appreciate your help."

"I'll do my best," Ben said. "That's all I'll promise. I figure James did the best he could too, and that's all anybody can ask."

James returned and brought a copy of the two easements along with addresses and phone numbers for the Bingham brothers and Dilbert Sweatt. The Bingham number was at Sand Hill and Sweatt was listed as living over at Waverly, twenty miles away. Ben examined the easements quickly and noted that TLC had legal right to enter the properties at any time and for any purpose. He also saw that the consideration paid was five dollars per pole, including surface damages, back in 1930. Damages done to the land in the future were negotiable when such an entry actually occurred.

"O.K.," Ben said, "this is all I need. I'll get out there and see what I can do. I'll call you as soon as I can. I appreciate the information James and I thank you for the coffee. Take care Roy. Both of you." Ben shook both men's hands as he prepared to go.

"You're welcome to my desk and phone if you want to call for an appointment," James said.

"I'd rather blind side them!" Ben said, "And if you happen to hear from any of those guys I don't want you to mention my name or that I'm looking for them. I'd like a promise from both of you on that."

Roy's face reddened, but both he and James nodded agreement. "Good luck Ben," Roy said. "You keep your seat James, we've got things to talk about!"

Ben closed the door softly, and within fifteen minutes he was at the Holiday Inn coffee shop with a Saint Aaron paper to read.

chapter xx

Sandhill is a four-block scab of shantytown resting in a sea of sand five miles east of Dry Lake and Ben had little difficulty in locating the Bingham house. As he stopped short of the hog wire fence he could see a man sitting on a decrepit old sofa on the shaded front porch. He walked to the front gate and greeted the seated figure. "Are you Mr. Bingham?"

"Which one are you looking for?"

"How many are there?"

"They's two of us—I'm Ed. My brother's name is Jed."

"Then I guess I need to talk to you Mr. Ed Bingham," Ben said, "but if Jed is around I'll talk to both of you."

"Are you peddling insurance or something? If you are, we don't need any," Ed said.

"I'm not selling anything."

"Well then, what do you want with us. I don't recognize you. Do you know Jed?"

"No, I don't live around here, I just need to talk to you for a few minutes. Name's Ben. I'm not here to waste your time or try to sell you anything."

"I am kind of busy," Ed admitted." I've got to go to the field directly and plow cotton. Damn thistles are taking over. Come on up and light, but I ain't got all day to set around and talk."

As Ben neared the porch a fawn colored, popeyed chihuahua stood up beside Ed Bingham and began to bark objections. Ben smiled and stepped onto the porch. The tempo of the yapping increased.

"That's a fine looking guard dog you've got there Mr. Bingham. Nobody's going to come in this yard without a challenge. Chihuahuas are the best watchdogs in the world I guess. What's its name?"

"This is Sugar," Ed picked the little dog up and placed him on his lap. "He belonged to my Mama."

"I've got one at home," Ben said. "Mine's named Pedro. He makes a lot of racket too, but I wouldn't take for him."

"How big is Pedro? Old Sugar weighs around five pounds," Ed said.

"Pedro is about that size," Ben said. "He's seven years old."

"Sugar is eleven. He stayed in bed down at Mama's feet, right up to the time she went away. Mama loved Sugar and Sugar loved Mama. When cancer finally took Mama, Sugar bit the Justice of the Peace when he come out to pronounce her dead. Couldn't help but be proud of him!"

"They're loyal little cusses," Ben admitted. "They'll take on a boar lion if one threatens the family. I figure they're about the smartest dogs in the world too. Pedro sleeps in the bed with me and my wife—right down at her feet—and he'll let you know if a car goes down the street after dark. He knows everything we say and when it gets bedtime we spell out 'bed' sometimes and here he'll come on the run. I guess they can spell too."

"That's a fact," Ed rolled his eyes and smiled broadly, "and I'll tell you something you may not believe—but it's the truth."

"What's that?"

"Like I said, when Mama went away and he bit that Justice of the Peace Sugar did something that I've never seen or heard tell of before. He went up and licked Mama's face and said just as plain as day 'I love you Mama'. I'll never forget that."

"I believe you," Ben said. "I've never heard of such, but I don't doubt it one bit."

"That's enough dog talk," Ed said. "What are you wanting to talk about Mr.—what did you say your name was?"

"I'm Ben Drill, I work for the light company, and I hear we're kinda crossways with you and your brother. I'm here to try and make peace."

"So that's it! You're another one of them damn electric company hands. Me and Jed has done and run off one of you smart alecs," Ed's smile had vanished.

"Yeah, I work for them. I'm here to see if there's some way to get back on your good side. We try to get along with everybody. Especially farmers and ranchers. I don't know what caused the trouble but I hope we can work it out."

"I'll tell you what made us mad," Ed said. "That tie wearing land agent of yours come traipsing out here and told us they had to do some work on that line you've got running across my cotton patch. I told him we had cotton up and growing, but he didn't give a damn! He showed me a piece of paper my daddy signed back in 1929, and said that they had the right to go into my field when they took a notion. He said he'd come back when they got through and pay me for what cotton they tore up. I asked him how much, and he said that he'd figure it out once the work was done. He made me and Jed mad as hell just the way he acted. Never even took off them damn sun glasses. Then they got out there and got one of their trucks stuck in that low place and ruined an acre of cotton trying to get the damn thing pulled out.

"I called that man and told him to get his ass out here and look at the mess they'd made, but he wouldn't come. He said he'd be back when the job was done—and not before.

"So, I run the whole damn bunch off and then that land agent called up and told me he was coming out with the Sheriff. I told him to come ahead, but he never showed up. So now they've sent you. Is the Sheriff on the way?"

"There'll be no Sheriff," Ben said. "You and me can work this out without a Sheriff. How about we go out and look at your field."

"Wake up and get out here Jed!" Ed yelled into the house. "Another one of them electric company hands is here!" Jed came out, rubbing his eyes and fastening the straps on his overalls. His hair was uncombed and he appeared to be a younger brother to Ed.

"It's a hell of a note when a man can't finish his nap," Ben said. "I'm sorry to wake you up."

Jed sat down and pulled on his boots, but he didn't speak or even look at Ben. It was easy to see that he considered the interruption a hell of a note too.

"Can we go in my car?" Ben asked.

"Not unless you want to walk back," Ed said. "Our field is deep sand and that Ford of yours would bury up like a doodle bug." Ed put Sugar inside the house and they walked to the rear of the house where a four-wheel drive army surplus weapon carrier was parked. Ed got under the wheel and Ben sat beside him in the front seat with his feet atop a sizable collection of empty beer cans. Jed climbed into the rear seat and lay down to finish his nap. He never showed his face again during the entire trip.

As Ed had reported his field was truly a "hell of a mess." The described fifty foot easement had been expanded to two hundred feet in several places, and in the low place Ed had spoken of, where the truck got stuck, it was wider than that. Ed, of course, had already seen the mayhem, but his outrage rekindled as he pointed out the damage.

"Them poles and junk is scattered all over the place too," Ed said. "They don't give a damn about my cotton crop.. Else they'd be a lot more careful!"

"Pretty sloppy," Ben admitted. "Looks like they had a time pulling that truck out."

Back at the house Ed and Ben returned to the porch. Ed left Jed asleep and said when he got hot enough he would wake up, hangover or not. Sugar came back out and reclaimed his place in Ed's lap. Ed sat silently and waited for Ben to say something.

"The way I see it, we're going to owe you for some cotton, some cleanup and some re-plowing. How much line do we have on your place?"

"It's a mile across it. The whole section is planted in cotton, and you can see it's looking good. If everything goes right and we get a little rain I'll make pert near a bale to the acre. They've ruint three acres already and they're only half way across me. I could lose five or six bales of cotton in this deal!"

"How much money is that?"

"Hard to say. Nobody can predict what cotton will bring, but it will be better than a hundred dollars a bale."

"How much would you charge for you and your tractor if you plowed for the public?"

"I don't plow for the public," Ed said. "It's about all I can do to keep my own farm."

"I know," Ben said, "but we've got to figure out what we owe you to get the ground we're driving and working on back in shape."

"With my furnishing the tractor and fuel I'd ask at least ten dollars an hour," Ed said," but like I say I don't plow for the public."

"I've got a proposition for you Mr. Bingham," Ben said. "You let our crew back on your place to finish their job. I'll write you a check for two hundred dollars, just to keep an eye on them and pull them out with your tractor in case they get stuck again. I'll have them haul the poles we replace out to your turn row and give them to you. They make good posts, especially for corners, when they're sawed to length. When they're all through with the rebuilding and the line is back in service I'll come back and pay you for the cotton you lost and the hours it takes to get your field in shape for next year. You may have to plow the tore up part twice, and I'm willing to pay you for doing it."

"How do I know you'll do what you're saying?" Ed asked.

Ben walked to his car and came back with his checkbook, sat back down and waited for a word from Ed.

"You're going to give me two hundred dollars to pull them out if they get stuck. Right?"

"That's our deal."

"Then you'll be back and pay me my cotton loss and the extra plowing when I market my cotton—at the same price I get at the gin. And, you'll let me have the posts you replace."

"Yep," Ben said. He wrote a check and handed it to Ed. Ed looked to be sure it was for two hundred dollars. He put it into the bib pocket of his overalls.

"How do I know you'll come back?"

"You got my word on it," Ben said, "and I'm going to write my name and home phone number down for you. If, you need to talk to me you won't be talking to a secretary. You'll be talking to me, my wife Flossie or my daughter Donna, and I want you to make it a collect call. Call at night or on weekends and I'm more likely to be home. If I'm not, my wife can find me. Do I have your word that you'll help us finish our work?"

"You do!" Ed extended his hand but Sugar arose and began to growl and bark. He was ready to attack.

"I'll take your word for it," Ben smiled, "I don't want to get dog bit. Tell Jed it was nice to meet him."

"Jed probably won't even remember you've been here," Ed said. "Them cans you had your feet in was emptied yesterday, and Jed did all the work hisself."

chapter XXI

"You can probably find him at the feed store. He goes up there every day of the world and plays moon. He'll come dragging back home in time to hear Paul Harvey at dinner time, so he won't be hard to find," Mrs. Dilbert Sweatt told Ben. He had not had much difficulty in locating the Sweatt home, thanks to directions which James Lemond had provided.

"I appreciate it," Ben said. "I've got a few errands to run, but I'll either catch Mr. Sweatt at the feed store, or come back by here. I hate to interrupt a moon game."

"You don't want to interfere with the Paul Harvey news either," Mrs. Sweatt said. "He won't even talk to me when that's on. You'd better make it back around one thirty. Can I tell him who's looking for him in case you miss him at the feed store?"

"My name's Ben Drill. I don't think I've ever met your husband. I need to visit with him, but I don't aim to butt into his moon game or Paul Harvey's program. I'll just show up here a little after one thirty." He could tell that the reason for his need to talk with Dilbert Sweatt was about to be questioned so he wasted no time in getting back into his car and back on the hard packed caliche road that led to the Interstate.

With two hours to kill, he had no intention of going to the Waverly Feed Store. Confronting a disturbed landowner in the company of his cronies was a tragic mistake that land agents make but once. Ben drove twenty miles and arrived at Miz Ethel's eating establishment in downtown Chalk Draw.

Miz Ethel's was a favorite of his and anytime he was within fifty miles of Chalk Draw he made it a point to eat there. The food was served boarding house style, at tables that would accommodate eight. Service began at eleven and lasted until around two. If you did not want to stand in line, or sit with a crowd you showed up at eleven, and finished your meal before the lines formed.

The decor lacked in elegance but the food made up for that shortcoming. Once seated, you were provided with a plate, a bowl, eating utensils, coffee or tea, and water. You were on your own from that point and helped yourself from steaming bowls of vegetables and meats until you reached the saturation point. Anytime the supply ran low, one of the army of waitresses replaced it with another brim full bowl of the same. The feeding frenzy wrapped up with most any dessert imaginable. Ben chose peach cobbler for his topper and downed two helpings.

There were only three others at the table and conversation was mercifully lacking, so Ben finished up by eleven fifteen, delivered his plate and silverware to the receptacle near the payout station and handed seven dollars to the cashier. Questioned, he testified that the food and service were top notch and left the building as the avalanche of diners began to arrive.

Dilbert Sweatt was waiting in the front yard when Ben drove in at one thirty five. He was tossing a ragged yellow tennis ball for his collie dog's amusement, but he stopped the play as Ben got out of the car.

"Mighty good looking dog you got there," Ben said as he extended his hand. "I'm Ben, and I guess you're Mr. Dilbert Sweatt. Your wife told me I'd probably be able to catch you a little after one thirty."

"Everybody calls me Bert," he clasped Ben's hand without emotion. "What do you want with me? I'm not in the market for anything, so if you're selling something you may as well look for a customer somewheres else."

"I couldn't sell hundred dollar bills for a nickel apiece Bert. I'm with the light company. I'm told that you're kinda put out with us."

"You got that right!" Bert kicked at the tennis ball. "Your damn company sent a pushy bastard out here last week and he really rubbed me the wrong way. If I had that man on my payroll I'd fire him!"

"Sometimes people see things different and it causes hard feelings. The man they sent out here regrets the way he disturbed you. He told me so himself."

"He didn't ask me if they could go on my place and work on their electric line—he told me they were going to do it. Then he got out his little brief case and showed me a map and a 1930 easement my daddy signed before they built it. Said they had the legal right and read me the line that said it. My old daddy signed that easement and got five dollars a post. They's ten of them in my pasture, and I'd give fifty dollars apiece to get them took off!"

"Did Mr. Lemond tell you that we'd pay you for damages when we finished the work?"

"He mentioned it," Bert admitted. "But he wouldn't say how much. I got him to spread out his map and we looked it over and he showed me how your outfit had put in exactly ten posts, but over at the east end your line turns right and goes into your power station and there's a damn guy wire there that ain't called for on the paper daddy signed. A cow or a horse could break its neck running into that guy wire, and it ain't even supposed to be there. It's a wonder some of my stock ain't been killed."

"Have you got time to run out there to the substation? We'll do better to look at it on the ground. I don't have one of those maps. I do better when I can see exactly what you're talking about."

"Suits me," Bert said. "I ain't got nothing better to do. Do you know what that guy that come out first told me?"

"No I don't," Ben said. "What did he say?"

"He said that the fact that guy wire ain't called for don't mean a damn thing! Said your outfit had the right for it by adverse possession or something like that. That's when I got mad and run him off."

"Will my car make it to the substation?" Ben asked. "Or will we have to walk in?"

"We'll go in my pickup," Bert said. "Them Ford cars hit high center running over a beer can. You meet me in town and we'll go in my pickup. I'll tell my wife where I'm going and meet you in front of the feed store. Don't go in there though, old man Funderburg will snoop into your business. He's the nosiest old devil in town."

Waverly substation was one of several 69-12.5KV substations connected to a TLC transmission line running from Dry Lake on the west to Blessing on the east. The transmission line furnished power for Waverly and the rural co-op tie in. Three distribution lines emanated and carried house power to the scattered load centers.

Bert drove to the north side of the substation and showed Ben the offending guy wire. It strengthened the dead end structure and conductor to the bus work and the transformer. The dead end structure was located on TLC property, but the guy wire went to ground on Bert Sweatt's side of the chain link fence.

"Do you see that damn guy wire? It's on my land, and your outfit ain't got no right to have it there." Bert said as they got out of his pickup truck.

"Looks like you're right about that," Ben admitted, "and you claim that guy don't show up on the map or the easement?"

"I've got both of them on my dash board. I'll get them and you can look at them for yourself. That guy that come out first gave me copies." Ben read the instrument and looked at the alignment map. The guy wire was not mentioned or pictured.

"I'm not a lawyer," Ben said, "but it looks like you're right Mr. Sweatt. I can't find any mention of that guy wire. But, do you know what would happen if it was removed?"

"I figure the whole mess would just cave in, and you'd be out of business," Bert smiled.

"You're right," Ben said. "We've got to have that structure guyed. You'd be out of business too. Your power comes from this substation. The co-op gets their power here."

"I've got a hack saw in my truck," Bert said. "And I've got a good notion to just saw that guy wire in two. I doubt you'd be able to seat a jury that would find fault with me for doing it!"

"I don't know about that," Ben said, "but you'd better wear welding goggles when you cut that guy wire. There's going to be the damndest flash of light you ever saw when that pole falls across that bus work. Kind of like getting struck by lightning. If you'll wait until after sundown they'll be able to see the fire works all the way to Dry Lake."

"I've got welding goggles," Bert said. "I'm much obliged for your advice and I'll wear them when I saw it off."

"You ought to have the fire department standing by too," Ben said. "Those broom weeds and dry grass will burn like coal oil after that transformer and those oil circuit breakers explode." Bert listened attentively and his resolve ebbed as he considered the impact his action might have. He re-folded his map and easement and put them into his back pocket. "You ain't just trying to scare me are you?" he asked.

"Nope," Ben said, "I've seen those lines go down and it's a sight you'll not ever forget. You ready to go back to town?"

As they climbed back into the pickup Bert had a lot of possibilities on his mind, and most of them were bad for him. His bluff had apparently failed. Ben did not appear to care whether he sawed that guy wire down or not.

"There might be a better way to solve this problem," Ben said.

"Would you consider fifty dollars to cover the guy wire and us giving you all the old poles we replace on your ranch? They make good corner and corral posts. They've got creosote enough in them to last another hundred years. The only weak place in them is at the ground line." Bert did not respond as they drove back to the feed store and Ben was also silent. As a matter of fact he leaned back and closed his eyes as Bert drove the three miles.

"Tell me again what your offer is," Bert said as Ben reached for the door handle. They were parked beside Ben's car and Bert had been thinking on the way to town.

"I'm offering fifty dollars and the poles we take out on your place if you'll give us the right to leave our guy wire in the ground," Ben said. "I've got my check book in the car and a sheet of paper you and me can write the deal down on. We'll both sign it, and it don't even have to be notarized. I'll trust you and you can trust me." They concluded their agreement on the hood of Ben's Tempo and Bert admitted that he'd been treated "like a man."

"When our crews are through with their maintenance I'll be back and pay for any surface damages and grass loss," Ben said. "I'm going to write my name and number on the agreement, and I'll mail you a copy back for your files."

"That smart aleck won't be coming in your place will he? I don't want him back out here."

"It will be me," Ben said, "unless I get killed in a car wreck or by a mad land owner." He grinned and the two shook hands.

"My brothers in law, old Ed and Jed Bingham are on the war path too," Bert confided. "Have you heard about that?"

"I've already been to see them," Ben said. "We worked it out."

Ben stopped for coffee at the On Site Delite, placed a call to Roy Glenn and told him that his crews could go back to work. He gave all the details Roy needed to know and asked that the word be passed on to Brad Hare. Roy expressed his gratitude and said that Brad would be told of developments. Ben got back on the Interstate and did not slow down until he pulled into his home driveway in Bo Dark. He hid his car in the garage, walked inside, turned on the television and lay down on the couch with Pedro, who licked his face and curled up beside him. They were both sound asleep in five minutes.

Chapter XXII

The front door opened and closed, but the rustle of paper grocery bags in the hall and Pedro's rousing to greet Flossie's arrival was the wake up call for Ben. He looked at his watch and was surprised to find he'd been sound asleep for more than two hours. Daytime naps of that length were rare.

"I didn't expect to find you here," Flossie said. "I didn't even know you were coming home. Especially since it's only Wednesday." She triggered the overhead light as she made her way to the kitchen and deposited her two sacks onto the counter top. Ben didn't rise until he heard the start up of Mr. Coffee.

"I got to a place where I can take off a day or two," Ben said. "I played out and decided that I needed a little R and R. I hid my car so no one would know I was here—then me'n old Pedro took us a siesta. Man I lust for a cup of home brewed coffee! How'd your day go? And, where is Donna? Shouldn't she be home from school?"

"If you took time to listen when you call home every once in a while you'd know that Donna has band practice every day after school," Flossie said as she searched for two clean cups. "I see she didn't have time to wash dishes before she left for school. I left them for her. I had to go to work before she got up."

Ben went to the kitchen shirtless and bare footed and, sat on a stool at the counter, dumped an overfilled ash tray into the plastic lined trash container and lit up. Flossie switched on the vent-a-hood to exhaust the smoke. She was a week deep in not smoking, but her resolve weakened when there was tobacco aroma in the area. Ben had forgotten that the filled ashtray was purposely left on the counter as a deterrent. He took one more puff and ground his cigarette out.

"You don't have to put your cigarette out," she said. "It don't bother me for you to smoke. If you want to die of cancer it's your business. I turned the vent-a-hood on so I won't have to die with you."

Flossie was a Registered Nurse and was employed at a re-hab center for drug, alcohol and tobacco addiction. She was not tempted by drugs or alcohol, but tobacco was a longtime habit, and she had fought the craving since she had earned her license at Austin a year ago. Sometimes a "quit smoking" lasted a week.

She'd waited until Donna was a sophomore before she enrolled in nursing school. Donna was now in her senior year at Bo Dark High, so Flossie's career had mainly been the raising of a daughter since she'd become Ben's bride back in 1950. At that time he was being recalled to the Army as a result of Harry Truman's decision to conduct a police action in Korea.

Ben, who had only been out of the Army for six months, used all the persuasive power at his command to convince Flossie to marry him before he reported for duty. She was not actually ready to settle down, but a week before he reported to Fort Hood, Texas; she became Mrs. Benjamin Arthur Drill. The Korean war was more persuasive in Margo "Flossie" Galloway's acquiescence than Ben Drill's pleadings.

He did not go to Korea. He was assigned to Special Services in the 2nd Armored Division and spent thirteen months at Fort Hood. Corporal Drill worked in the supply room and at the post movie theaters. He popped, sacked and sold popcorn. He and Flossie rented a small two room apartment on the second floor of a rooming house in downtown Killeen, since you had to be a sergeant or better to qualify for on base housing.

Following his discharge, the couple migrated to Vast Plain, Texas, where Ben was employed by Texas Lighting Company. Vernon Marmaduke, Division Engineer of the Transmission Department hired him and told him he was to be a right of way agent. Ben did not know what a right of way agent was, but he jumped at the chance and had been on the payroll in that capacity since 1952. He'd worked in the part of West Texas, which lies between Blessing and El Paso. Donna had been born in 1967.

Vernon Marmaduke advanced up the coporate ladder and in 1967 he was named President and General Manager for TLC in Metroplex. Ben and Flossie followed in 1970. The area of his responsibility remained the same, but now he drove three hundred miles to work. Normally he left home on Monday morning, worked out of a motel room and came home on weekends. Some weekends.

Until Burkeen had his car wreck, Brown died and Gankle was

claimed by retirement Ben had been relatively content with his job. When he wound up as the last man standing, early retirement beckoned and Ben would qualify on his fifty-fifth birth date, in January of 1985! He'd made up his mind to get out of the game. Retirement benefits were reduced, but he got to keep his life and insurance benefits. He had no plans past getting off the road, but there'd be time for planning when he bought his final tract of land.

Flossie put his coffee before him and they were both sipping when Donna roared into the driveway and braked to a screeching stop. The Ford Mustang engine was loud with the hollow muffler, but it was drowned out by the radio. She had a Dairy Queen coke in her hand, and slammed the door when she entered the house. Pedro rushed to meet her and she picked him up and kissed him.

"How's my boy," she said as she came back to the kitchen. "Hi Dad-O!" she greeted Ben. She also kissed him on the cheek. "When did you get home? Mom, I didn't have time to do the dishes this morning—I'm cramming for final exams, so I can graduate from that hell hole of a school in June, but I'll do them in the morning. Okay?"

"I got in about middle of the evening," Ben said. "Why don't you go ahead and do the dishes now?"

"Don't have time," she said. "Derek is picking me up in thirty minutes. He's taking me out to the movie. But," she added, "I'll be home by eleven."

"You've promised to do those dishes for two days," Flossie said. "I'm going to hold you to it—they'll still be there when you get up in the morning. You'll need to put the trash out too."

"No problem," Donna said as she put Pedro back on the floor. "You going to spend the night at home Dad-O?"

"I plan on it," Ben said. "I want you to tell me about this guy Derek?"

"He's out of high school. You'll like him a lot, but he won't have time to come in. We've got to hurry so we won't miss the start of the movie. I'll talk to you in the morning. Goodnight Mom, Dad-O! I'll make Derek drive slow." Donna went down the hall to her room with Pedro trailing along behind.

"What do you think of this Derek?" Ben asked as he reached for the cigarettes in his shirt pocket. He remembered in time to not bring them out. Flossie noticed and smiled.

"Not much," she said. "Derek's out of school by request. He was expelled for some reason, but Donna won't say why. She says that he was in the right though, and was set up by the Principal just to get rid of him. I think he was caught smoking on the school ground—and he was not smoking anything you can buy over the counter the way I heard it."

"Well, by God I want to talk to Donna about that! I don't want her hanging out with any pot smoking troublemakers. Be right back." He felt Flossie's hand on his arm and he did not rise.

"That's the worst thing you could do," she said quietly. "The more you interfere with a couple their age the more determined they'll be to stay together. All we can do is hope for the best and pray that she sees that Derek is no good!"

"You're the one who's home with her, and I trust your judgment, but I worry about you two when I'm gone. You working over there with the crazies and her running around with one of your next crop of patients. Sometimes, I think the whole damn world has gone crazy! George Orwell tried to warn us that 1984 would be a bad year!"

A car braked to a stop at the curb, the front door slammed and Ben peeked through the separated slats of the blind as Donna got into a jet black Camaro with dark tinted glass. The tires squealed and they rocketed away.

"I couldn't even see him," Ben complained as he returned to his stool. "That car look's like it belongs to a gangster. How often do they date?"

"Two or three nights a week. If she's not in by eleven she's grounded for a week. So far she's been home on time."

Ben went out and bought pizza for supper, then cleared the table of the sacks and cartons. He saved a piece of crust for Pedro, who growled thanks and ran down the hall to hide it in a secret place.

Flossie and Ben half watched TV and talked during commercials until ten o'clock. Flossie announced that she was going to "b-e-d", but Pedro understood and began to run in circles to hurry her up.

"I've got to be at work by six," Flossie said. "Will you be at home this weekend?"

"I hope so," Ben said. "If nothing slips, tears or breaks. I've got to be in Chalk Draw early Monday. Five guys are coming into engineering and train to buy right of way. And, it's about time—I'm used up."

"Are you going to train them?"

"No way," Ben said. "They can learn the same way I did! But I'll be out there with them. I can't think of any way to get out of it. But it won't be long before I'll have a way."

"Big Daddy will talk you out of it. He's not going to let you retire until he's good and ready!"

"He'd better start getting ready," Ben said as he pulled his pack of Raleighs from his pocket. "I may smoke one outside before I come to bed." Wordlessly Flossie rose and she and Pedro vanished down the hall. Ben went out onto the patio and smoked three cigarettes. Back inside he watched the weather forecast. He turned the vent-a-hood off, left the entry hall light on and felt his way down the hall to the bedroom.

He quietly slid into the king size bed and rolled over toward Flossie. Pedro roused and barked a stern warning from his position at Flossie's side.

"What are you doing?" she said. "I've got to get some rest. I work long hours and I've got to be there at six in the morning. Leave Pedro alone and go to sleep." She turned to her side and patted Pedro.

Ben did as he was told.

chapter XXIII

Ben was roused from a deep and untroubled sleep by Pedro, who was standing beside him and barking for attention. Flossie had gone to work and left him responsible for seeing that Pedro was admitted to the great outdoors. They made it to the patio door without Pedro springing a leak and he ran outside to greet the day and water the grass. Ben shambled into the kitchen and poured a steaming draught from Mr. Coffee who had been left on "warm".

A glance at the clock told Ben that he'd slept until eight thirty and the quiet of the house told him that he and Pedro were alone. Flossie was at work, and hopefully Donna was at school. It was evident that neither had managed to wash any dishes before they left. Pedro barked and Ben let him back into the house and lifted him onto the couch. He burrowed into his afghan and made himself comfortable. Ben sipped three cups of coffee while he read the two-page span of comics and struggled with the New York Times crossword. He could master that crossword on Monday, Tuesday and Wednesday, but it was Thursday and he soon gave up and deposited the Star Telegram into the trash. He found the wire twists, secured the tops of all three bags, went back to the bedroom, found his pants and shirt and barely made it to the curb before the trash truck.

The lawn had not been mowed for two weeks, so Ben ran the mower over both the front and back. Then he went into the house and washed dishes until ten o'clock. He put them away, vacuumed the kitchen area and turned the television on, but it had no offering that got his interest. He shaved and showered, checked Pedro's water and food dish and drove to the Hwy Robery Cafe for breakfast and more coffee. Being home alone was not a situation that Ben enjoyed, and he sometimes wondered what life would be like if he took early retirement. He'd be fifty-five, his daughter would be gone and his wife had already told him that she was going to keep working.

"You'll be fifty five," she said, "but I'll only be fifty. I stayed home and raised Donna, before I got my RN license and now it's my turn to be out of the house. You can stay here, or do whatever you want to, but I enjoy my job and I'm going to keep it!"

Giving up his job at TLC would most likely add years to his life, but Ben did not enjoy washing clothes and dishes while the Young and the Restless or Lucy re-runs furnished background music. Retirement was a big step, with a down side. The rambling fever Merle Haggard sang about might actually be incurable, and Ben fretted that he might not know it until too late.

"Hey neighbor, what in the hell are you doing home on a Thursday?" Ben looked up from his short stack and Cecil Short smiled as he seated himself across the table and signaled for a cup of coffee.

Cecil lived on the same block as Ben. His wife Marie worked for the railroad while Cecil roamed the area and dealt in experienced automobiles and pickup trucks. Marie did all the household maintenance and cooked the meals for her enterprising husband. Cecil slept late, ate his lunch away from the house and was always dressed suitable for framing. He bought second hand rolling stock, but he did not dirty his hands in the restoration process. He hired that done and always seemed to come out on the profitable side in his dealings. Cecil had retired when Marie agreed to become his third wife and in their seven years of residency in Bo Dark Cecil had never held a steady job. Some of the locals gossiped that Cecil was a con artist, some said he was just plain lazy, but the majority reserved judgment until additional evidence was discovered. Cecil had told Ben that he didn't give a damn what people thought.

"Haven't had a day off for three weeks," Ben responded. "They've run me ragged lately so I gave myself a few days off. What have you been up to?"

"I just bought an El Camino pickup," Cecil said. "Got it an estate sale and bought it right. I've got it in the body shop for a little bondo and a coat of paint. Then I'll start looking around for it a good home. If you're in town the next couple of weeks you might want to look at it. It'll be priced worth the money."

"We're starting a big job next Monday," Ben said. "I never know when I'll be home for sure. I'd like to look it over, but don't pass up a sale waiting on me."

"Don't worry about that," Cecil smiled. "Once that baby's got it's new coat it can be bought. I don't get any sentimental attachment to rolling stock."

"I've been considering taking my retirement next year," Ben said as he pushed his plate to one side. "Have you got any wisdom to pass along on how to deal with retirement?"

"How the hell would I know anything about retirement," Cecil bristled. "I work every day just like you do. I ain't about to set around that house and watch television, or mow the lawn, or paint. If I did stuff like that I'd a been dead ten years ago. Hell, I'm sixty years old but I damn sure ain't considering retirement."

As Ben paid out for his breakfast Cecil migrated to a table with three men and an empty chair. He began his spiel on the El Camino.

Back home, he was letting Pedro outside when the phone rang. Ben ignored the first ten rings, but finally decided that it might be Donna or Flossie. After all, they were the only ones who knew that he was home. It was not Donna, and it was not Flossie. The caller was Ruby.

"Just making a pit stop," Ben lied. "What do you need?"

"For openers," she said, "I need to hear from you every day so that we'll know where you are. Brad gets huffy with me when I can't locate you."

"Simmer down," Ben said. "I've been kind of busy and it hasn't been handy to call in. Besides all that I don't have anything to report. Does Brad need to talk?"

"He's gone somewhere right now. I've called a dozen motels looking for you!"

"Do you know what the big emergency is? I'm only going to be at home for a little while. I've got to go down south and check on the construction crew. See if they've got flooded out again."

"One of your clients, Mr. Gaither in the Sulpher Draw community is furious about a pecan tree our construction crew pulled over on his place. The pecan tree was not even on the right of way. His phone number is ....," Ruby paused and Ben could hear the rustling of paper. "I guess I left it on my desk. Hang on while I go to my desk and find it. I'm in Brad's office."

"I won't need it," Ben said. "I remember Mr. Gaither and know exactly where he lives. He's on our High Bank line and I can be there way before dark. I'll be on the road soon as we hang up. Tell Brad not to worry about it. I'll handle it and call back."

"There's something else you need to know too."

"What's that?"

"I'm filing for a divorce," Ruby sobbed. "Don hit me last night!"

That item of news aroused Ben much more than Gaither's fallen pecan tree but he tried to remain calm. As he paused and searched for a suitable response he could hear Ruby sobbing softly. At least, she was in Brad's office and it was not likely that she would be overheard.

"Why did he hit you?" He finally asked.

"He thinks I'm slipping around on him?"

"Did you admit it?"

"Of course not! But I'm going to file for divorce tomorrow morning. I wish I was with you right now. We could make things all better."

"I don't know about that," Ben said, "but I'm sorry to hear about your trouble. You might want to think about it awhile before you do anything foolish and mess up your and Chrissie's life."

"I can't go on living with a man who accused me of slipping around and then hit me. I want to be with you Ben. I need to see you."

"This weekend and all next week I'll be so tied up I doubt we can manage it," Ben said. "I think it would be a bad idea anyway. What if he actually catches you? He'll probably wind up with custody of Chrissie in a divorce action."

"I hadn't thought of that," Ruby admitted. "You may be right, but I need so much to see you."

"We can talk by telephone," Ben said, "and that will probably be the smart way to handle things right now. The last thing we need to happen is for Don to find out about you and me."

"You're probably right," Ruby sobbed. "But he's not coming back in my house. He's not going to hit me and get by with it!"

"Do what's best for you and Chrissie," Ben said. "A divorce is a serious thing. You might need to think awhile before you actually split the blanket."

"I'll think about it," Ruby promised between sobs, "but I don't see any way for me to ever live with Don after he's hit me!"

"I've got to get on the road," Ben said. "I'll report in tomorrow. Until then, think about you and Don and little Chrissie and what a divorce could do to your lives."

"I'll try. Be careful on the road. I love you!" Ben cradled the phone without responding and was out the front door before she had time to call back.

Chapter XXIV

Wilbur Gaither raised and sold registered Palomino horses for pleasure and profit on his five hundred acres of prime grassland in the Sulfur Draw community. He and wife Grace owned the place free and clear and lived in a fieldstone home located near the center of that acreage. Native grass grew stirrup deep in the low places and water seeped from live springs. It pooled in several dammed up ponds in the draws, and although it had a sulphurous odor, the horses did not seem to mind the smell or taste. Sulphur water has a reputation of being healthful, and Will and Grace Gaither had a deep well and a submersible pump that provided water for the house. Ben remembered that he was not really all that fond of that water or the coffee brewed from it, but he'd kept his judgement to himself when he bought right of way for the 138KV wood pole H frame line.

Those negotiations had been a little different than most, in that Will and Grace did not speak to each other, although they'd been man and wife for over forty years.

From the entry hall you took a left turn to visit with Will, but Grace lived in the area to the right. Those arrangements puzzled Ben, but he was not puzzled sufficiently to ask any questions.

Both had signed the easement and Ben had written separate checks, but at no time were the three in the same room. Grace admitted that Mr. Gaither had a good head for business and that she would abide by any agreement that he and Ben made.

"You get Mr. Gaither's signature on your paper, and show it to me and I will sign," she had said. That was precisely the sequence of events at the Gaither place.

It had been an easy and pleasant negotiation once Ben had convinced Will that he was receiving the same money as his neighbors. In addition, Will and Grace had received a hundred dollars each for seven bearing size pecan trees that grew in one of the draws. They were native pecan trees, with nuts the size of an acorn. Will did not spray the trees and half the nuts had wormholes. The other half were not harvested, but deer and squirrels saw that they did not go to waste. Will said the trees' value were as shade for his horses.

As Ben neared the house he saw the rear of Mrs. Gaither's Cadillac through the open door to her garage, but there was no pickup beneath the liveoak on Will's side of the house. "Damn," Ben said. He feared that he'd made a two-hour drive for nothing. Will was probably off somewhere showing his horses.

A glance at the barn though and Ben spotted the pickup. He did not stop at the house. Will was inside drinking a sweating can of Bud. He was seated on a bale of costal hay, and motioned for Ben to join him.

"Howdy, amigo," Will did not rise from his bale of hay. "Rise and light—have a cool one with me if it ain't contrary to your scruples. I've got a case iced down in the box."

"I got word that we've done you some hurt Mr. Gaither," Ben said as he sat down on a bale facing him. "I came right on out here soon as I got word."

"I disremember who you are," Will admitted. "I thought you might need a good horse. Get yourself a beer. It will go down easy, cause it's might near froze. Kind of like one of them orange slushes."

Ben glanced at his watch and saw that it was only four fifteen. He would not usually consider drinking a beer during working hours, but today had been a day that justified departure from normal rules. He took a can from the refrigerator and pulled the tab. He was thirsty, but he had no craving for sulphur water.

"Looking for a horse?" Will asked. "I've got some dandies!"

"I don't straddle horses younger than me," Ben smiled, "but palominos are my favorite breed—even though I don't think a whole lot of Roy Rogers. I work for the light company and I'm told that our contractor ruined one of your pecan trees. They said it was not on the right of way."

"That's a fact," Will admitted. "I caught the boy that was running that bulldozer right after he pulled it over."

"Pulled it over? How did he pull it over?"

"With a chain. Looked like a logging chain. He got his dozer stuck and tried to winch out by tying off to that tree. If his chain had been ten foot shorter that tree would have wiped him and that dozer both out!"

"We hired a contractor to build our line," Ben said, "but we accept liability for the damage both on and off the right of way. We can't stand that tree back up, but we can sure as hell pay you for it. I told you when we traded I'd be back when the line was charged and the job was over with."

A colt walked over and put his velvet muzzle against Ben's shirt pocket. He slobbered on his shirt.

"Git away from here Sparkle," Will threw his almost empty can at the colt. "He's a big pest," he smiled proudly. "Another year and he'll be worth a thousand dollars. Right now I've made him rotten and spoiled for sugar cubes."

Will fumbled with the snap on his shirt pocket and produced a cube of sugar. Sparkle responded quickly and gingerly removed it from Will's open palm. Satisfied for the moment the colt walked away.

"I told that operator that you were going to come back and pay damages when they got all through," Will said. "I don't know who he talked to or who called you, but it wasn't me. As far as I'm concerned you ain't due back here until they finish. That blade operator told me that would be another month or two even if the weather stayed good. I hate you had to come all this way for nothing. It must have scared that boy when he pulled the tree over."

"Possibly," Ben agreed, "some people would be madder than a wet hen in a circumstance like this. I can figure out something on the tree if you've got time to go look at it—or we can wait until our job's done."

"We'll wait." Will said. "Hell that old tree ain't made a pecan in thirty years and they weren't much bigger than an English pea when it was in its prime. The only thing I regret is losing the shade." Ben finished his beer, rose and arched his back to ease the nagging pain. He put the empty into a barrel that would soon need emptying.

"That would be handier—waiting I mean. That way we can settle up on everything all at one time." Ben raised his hands in refusal of another beer. "I really need to get on down the road. Here it is Friday and I aim to go home for the weekend. Might take my wife and daughter out to supper and treat them to a picture show."

"They doing okay?" Will inquired politely.

"Fine, fine," Ben said, "and how is Mrs. Gather?"

"Still crazy as hell," Will said. "Sets in her part of the house playing that damn piano and singing religious songs. But you don't want to hear my troubles. I'll see you when you get back this way."

"You don't want to hear my troubles either," Ben said as he patted Sparkle on the rump, shook Will's entended hand and walked to his car.

"Thanks for the beer," Ben called as he backed out, turned and headed back toward the highway.

Will was sitting back on his hay bale, fumbling for another sugar lump when Ben lost sight of him in the rear view mirror.

Chapter XXV

Ben waited at a corner table in the back dining room. It was a round table which would seat six and provide privacy for the expected crew. Kent was the first to arrive and was ushered back by the desk clerk. As he sat down Ben folded his newspaper and lit a cigarette.

"Did you get all fixed up last week?" Ben asked. He noted that Kent was dressed for the job. He wore Levi's that had made several trips through the washer, a tan western shirt and scuffed boots. Ben liked what he saw. The waitress came with coffee, topped Ben's cup and poured a starter for Kent, who said he'd wait awhile before ordering breakfast. He lit a Marlboro.

"Yeah, they got us all rigged up with transportation, an operating advance, calling cards, aerials and six hundred and seven survey permission sheets. I've got all the stuff in my car. Brad said you'd split it up and tell us how to get started. He says you'll be managing the project," Kent said.

"Yeah, that's what he told me too, but, I'm not a supervisor, and don't want to be. You'll all be on your own, that's the way this business works. Nobody can tell you what to say to a landowner, and you can't tell what a landowner might say to you. No two are exactly the same. But I guarantee you that better than half of them don't want an electric line across their place. You can count on that.

"So don't be surprised if one of them runs you off. And, try not to make one so mad that you can't go back. Put yourself in his place and you probably wouldn't want a transmission line across your back yard, field, or pasture either."

"I kinda understand that," Kent said. "Me and Harold and Bob got a distribution line easement signed once in a while when a customer asked for service. Even when they request a line and need electricity they're hard to please. I don't think J. J. has ever got an easement, and

I know that Bill hasn't. He was local manager at Ringer, but from what he says he was mostly a glad hander."

"Well," Ben said, "The principal's the same whether it's distribution voltage or 345KV. It takes lines to deliver power, and the higher the voltage the bigger the line. It's one thing to have a line built on your place so you can have service, but it's a different proposition when a steel tower line crosses your place that you can't even tap into. Everybody wants electricity but damn few want a line!"

"Well," Kent said, "I hired on with this outfit to make a living for me and Lilly, and I mean to retire with a monthly income and hospitalization. I'm in for the long haul and will do whatever it takes to get there—no matter what the job is. I'll need help. I know that, but I don't plan to depend on you to do my thinking or tell me what to say."

"I'll work with you guys," Ben smiled, "but you won't work for me—and I won't work for you. We're all out here with Brad Hare to satisfy, and all he wants is a place to build lines. He don't really care how you get it, but he don't like to be lied to or catch anybody not carrying their own weight. He'll back you to the hilt if you play square with him. I'll guarantee you that!"

"That's what he said about you." Kent said, "and he told us that you'd do your fair share."

Within the next thirty minutes the four others arrived. Bill came in last. He'd missed the turn off ramp and had to go two miles before he found a place to double back. He was dressed in a suit and tie and looked out of place because of it, but he was comfortable with his appearance. His wife had chosen his outfit.

Bob wore khaki pants and a pale pink, loose fitting shirt that looked slept in. He was definitely not a clotheshorse, but he wouldn't stick out in a crowd. His footwear was penney loafers, and they'd been around for awhile.

Hal wore his drumming outfit, which was gaudy C&W, and he sported glossy black Justin boots. Pimp pumps was what he called them.

J. J. was the undisputed standout in the wardrobe department. His western shirt was blood red, brand new and his jeans were not the off the rack variety. A 'J. J.' brand was embroidered over his left shirt pocket and on the right rear pocket of his jeans.

He'd been able to locate his Red Raider boots and they were tipped with silver. He'd bought them when he was a student at Texas Tech University many years ago. Opportunities to wear red boots are rare, so they were in mint condition. He'd lasted two years at Tech before he hired on as summer help at TLC. He met Nancy Partain and made a wise marriage.

"You're looking cool," Hal said, "and if you happen to lose your shirt or britches they'll be easy to find with your brand on them." Everyone laughed, except J. J.

"I've got a room rented," Ben said. "Let's eat and take all that stuff Kent's got over and divide it up. They showed you the whole mess last week I figure." All nodded assent.

Ben's room had two beds and they provided ample space for the stacks of paper. There was a set of aerial photographs with the proposed line drafted in red ink. The tracts were designated with a dashed yellow boundary and an identifying tract number keyed to a typewritten list of the tract owners. Survey permission pages were included and Ben separated them into equal segments.

Each stack included aerials, an ownership list and permission sheets. The owner tally divided out with each man receiving one hundred and one owners to locate. Ben put the odd one in his pile and brought his share to a hundred and two.

"Now," he said, "I've thought about how we should fan out and go to work. Since I've got a job to finish out west I'm going to take that last bunch. I'll be staying in Vast Plain or Midway. Kent will stay in Dry Lake. Bill will stay here in Chalk Draw with Hal. J. J. can get a place in Blessing to work his section and Bill can headquarter over at Groom. That way we'll all be handy to our section of line. Sound reasonable?"

Each agreed to the plan and collected his paper work, then waited expectantly for whatever else Ben might say.

"Can't tell you exactly how to get survey permission," he lit a cigarette and sat on the corner of the dresser, "but I'll tell you how I'm going to try and get my part."

"I'd like to hear it," J. J. sat on the bed.

"First off," Ben said, "I'll drive all the roads that cross my section and figure out about where the line will cross. You can guess pretty close from your aerial maps.

"Then pick a likely place to start. A tract with a residence is a good place to begin, and your first contact is mighty important. Even if you don't get survey permission you might learn something about the next landowner you need to contact. It's real important to leave everyone in a good mood.

"I tell them who I work for, and that I'm asking for permission for a survey crew to cross their land. The survey is for the possible installation of an electric line, but I don't offer any more details than I have to. I don't try to impress anybody with my importance, my title or my knowledge.

"I emphasize that they're not giving us any right to build a line when they allow us to survey. If the route is picked by our engineers, I tell them that I'll come back and talk to them, but I don't speculate on how much we'll be paying if their land is involved. I've found that the least amount of detail you volunteer, the better off you are when you come back waving an easement.

"Of course, they need to know that the survey crew will drive wooden stakes, and sometimes cut a brush line, but any damage will be paid for that results from our crossing. And be sure and give them a way to get ahold of you in case something goes wrong. Like, if the surveyor leaves a gate open and a cow gets out. That's not likely, but you sure need to get that landowner or tenant's confidence at that first meeting. It's ninety nine percent certain that a line will be erected exactly where that aerial shows.

"Don't be in a hurry to get an owner to sign before he's ready. Rushing him can get you in trouble. If he needs to think, you let him think about it. Let him tell you when to come back. We've got time, around a month I think, and we sure as hell don't want to make enemies at this stage of the game. Think of this contact as an introduction and leave a good taste in their mouth, because you'll be going back to buy an easement, and settle damages. Nobody else will mess with your clients. They're yours until the project is complete.

"I'm probably repeating things you were told during your week at the office, so I'm going to shut up and figure you're ready to go to work. I'll be at Ramada Inn in Vast Plain this week. You will be in the locations I've named and in the motel of your choice. The work hours are up to you.

"Since Chalk Draw is about the midway point we'll meet here every Monday around nine o'clock and have a get together like this. That way we'll all know how we're doing. Any questions?"

"I have one," J. J. said. "Do we co-ordinate our job with the local managers of the town we're working near. In my years in Employee Benefits I've met and been involved with most of them on occasion. They might be of help to us, since they will be acquainted with people we're going to be calling on. Does that make sense to you Ben?"

"It's a bad idea to get involved with the locals," Ben said. "That's about the worst thing you can do! Sure as hell they'll have friends and maybe even relatives you may be calling on and the first thing that will happen is some local manager will be asking special treatment for his cronies. And, if you get trapped into that the other people along the line will find out. That puts you in a hell of a spot. I've been there! It's my policy to stay away from all local TLC employees. After the job you'll be gone, but they'll still be here, and innocent if something goes wrong. Some of the old timers had rather not even know you're in town. Brad Hare will tell them what he wants them to know about construction in their division."

"I see," J. J. said, but he did not say whether he would abide with the advice. It seemed to make sense to the other men and Bill admitted that in his years as local manager he'd never met a general office land buyer, "and I appreciated it," he admitted. "TLC had a couple of condemnations west of Ringer and I was glad I wasn't involved. Nobody was mad at me when it was over with." He gathered his maps and papers and Ben walked to his vehicle with him. On the way Bill thanked him for giving him the line beginning point, which was within fifty miles of Ringer.

"I can drive home if I need to, and that will be a comfort to Florence until she gets used to me being away from home at night. I haven't been away over two nights in a row since we've been married, and that's been a long, long time," Bill said. "I'll do my best to get that survey permission in a hurry. I'm just glad I've still got a job."

"You'll do fine," Ben said. "Just be careful what you say—and if you run into a hardcase just back off and go for the neighbors. Somebody has to be the last one to grant survey permission and will most likely be the last easement you buy too. Don't worry about not getting permission your first visit. You've been a local manager and I know you can buy right of way. Let the office know which motel you check into. Ruby keeps up with your location."

Bill climbed into his brand spanking new baby blue Chevy, rolled down the glass and thanked Ben again.

"Good looking rig," Ben said. He turned away and Bill backed out and headed for the Interstate.

"See you next Monday!"

J. J. was leaving, and he nodded as he exited the parking lot. He had a Stetson hat on his head, and he looked a little like Roy Rogers. Ben smiled at his urge to yell "Happy Trails" and nodded back.

Hal and Bill were on their way to the office to arrange for rooms. Ben told them that one of them could just transfer to his room. He'd arranged the reservation with that in mind.

"See you next Monday," Ben said. "Be careful and good luck."

"Where do you recommend over at Dry Lake?" Kent asked.

"The Home Place is as good as any," Ben said. "They've got big rooms, the television is fair and there's a twenty four hour restaurant. It's handy to the Interstate too."

"Let's meet some night this week. I'll come to Vast Plain or you can come over to Dry Lake. I'll buy supper. I've got a good expense account," Kent said.

"We'll do it," Ben smiled. "You've got a new car too so I'll let you drive to Vast Plain. I'll be in room 123 at the Ramada around six. I'll let you buy."

"O.K., I'll be there."

Ben went back into the room, gathered his paperwork and put it into the trunk of his car.

He placed a call to the office of Christopher Finn and learned that his easements had been received and were awaiting execution. Next he called the office and Ruby answered.

I'm at Ramada Inn in Vast Plain," Ben reported, "and you can tell Brad that I took care of our problem out at the Gaither place. Everything else running smooth?"

"Yes," she said. "I didn't file those papers. I can call back if you need to talk. I have another call."

"I'm leaving," Ben said, "I think you made the right decision."

Ben removed his boots, called the motel clerk and left instructions not to be disturbed. Then he switched on the television and lay down for his mid-day nap.

chapter XXVI

"Mr. Kelly, you spoke the gospel truth when you told me that your new neighbor is one of a kind. She beats anything I ever saw! She must have more beasts and birds than anybody in the county. And, they've all got names too." Ben wisely reserved his opinion of Frances Holiman's bizarre appearance and strange behavior. Goose smiled and held both hands up for Ben's inspection. They were near ordinary size and the regular color had returned.

"She's different," Goose said. "She thinks a little different than most, but I took to her right off when they run that piece in the paper about her. I guess you missed that article in the Telegram last year."

"Yeah, I missed it. I was working up around High Bank most of last year, so I didn't see the story. What kind of article was it anyway?"

"They was widening one of them main streets over in Midway," Goose recalled," and Miss Holiman's house had to be moved. They had to have her lot to make that street as wide as they wanted to. She wouldn't sell to them, so they took her to court. Towns can do just like your company. If they get it in their head to take some land, they can do it."

"I guess they condemned the property," Ben said. "I always hate to hear about that kind of deal, but it happens. Progress can sure cause hardship sometimes."

"Them high rollers in Midway was glad the road widening took in the Holiman place. They'd been looking for a way to get rid of her for years. She didn't look and act to suit a lot of people. Especially her neighbors. She took in too many cats and dogs, and all the ordinances was against her. They thought they had her by the short hair, when the picture they run in the Telegram showed her out on the front gallery with a ten gauge double barrel, and a bulldozer pulled up to her fence. The operator left it running when he saw her and that shotgun and thought of something he needed to do downtown. The police throwed up a barricade around her house, but they couldn't decide exactly what they ought to do next. They had on their bulletproof clothes, but they didn't charge the house or anything. She stood out on that porch with all her cats, dogs and that ten gauge until the Mayor came out. He didn't much want to, but he was up for re-election so he gutted up and acted brave. She stopped him at her front gate, and had him looking down both barrels.

"He told her the city had taken her property and that her money was down at the city clerk's office. He said they'd allowed a hundred thousand dollars for her land. All she had to do was come and pick it up.

"She told him that was for the land, but it didn't include her house the way she understood it. And she said she'd shoot anybody that tried to bulldoze her home.

"The Mayor told her he'd need to study that over and talk to the council about it. Said he'd be back in a couple of days, and promised her house wouldn't be pushed in the meantime. They moved their dozer.

"Made me so blamed mad I got Chris Finn to go to Midway and do something to help that woman—and send me the bill!

"I really don't know how he managed it, but he convinced the city to pull in their horns and give Miss Holiman time to find a place to move her house to. And that's where I come in. I made up my mind to help her and decided to make her a deal on the section she's on now. Chris handled it all and even got her house moved out of Midway. He hooked the city into footing the bill for the move, too.

"They took all them bricks off, numbered them some way and then re-installed them when they got the house moved out here.

"Miss Holiman hauled her cats and dogs out to the new place and commenced to add to her collection. Her inventory runs into more varmints than you can count.

"The city didn't get sued, the Mayor got reelected and Chris Finn had a high old time putting them Midway bastards in their place. He handled it as a personal favor and gave me a ten percent discount on his legal work. Everybody wound up winners—including me! Miss Holiman's a good neighbor. She don't bother nobody, and nobody better bother her. If they do, they're liable to catch hell from me and Christopher Finn."

"That's an amazing story," Ben said. "I'd been wondering how in the world you were talked into selling a square mile of real estate."

"Do you know what I got for that section?" Goose smiled as he relished the memory.

"I got no idea," Ben admitted.

"Come on in the house and I'll show you," Goose climbed the steps, picked his footing across the porch and opened the door. Ben followed and both climbed into their barber chairs.

"It ain't really any of my business what your land sold for," Ben said. "I don't mean to pry or put you on the spot."

"I want you to know Mr. Drill. Course, I'd like for you to keep it to yourself. I don't trust many people with knowing what I do. My lawyer frowns on my sharing too much information with the public. He's real touchy about some of the things I do."

"Whatever you tell me won't be repeated to anybody—anywhere," Ben looked straight into the eyes of Goose Kelly. "I didn't even tell anybody about your racing turtle. And, by the way, how's he doing?"

"He's primed and ready to get me a brand new pickup," Goose smiled. "I'll let you look at him before you get away. Now, what do you think of what I got for my land?"

"You didn't tell me."

"You're setting in half of it!"

"You mean to tell me that you swapped a square mile of land for two barber chairs?" Ben gasped.

"Exactly!" Goose said, "and I threw in half the minerals so's she'd have money enough coming in to feed her livestock. My brothers and sisters had a wall-eyed fit, but there ain't a damn thing they can do about it. I got the power of attorney, fifty one percent of the title, and the lawyer's on my payroll." Goose ratcheted his chair back a couple of clicks and relished the recall.

"That's a great story!" Ben said.

"Would you take seven hundred dollars, even, for each tower that is installed across your place? I went right to the throne room with your proposal and was finally able to ootch our offer higher. It's the best I can do looks like. But I can tell you that I can make up some of the difference after our construction is done and I come back to settle damages."

Actually, Ben had not even mentioned the negotiating stalemate to Wiley Kiel or Brad Hare. Acquiring the right of way was the only thing they were worried about. He could just as easily have paid what Goose had asked last time, but that would have been contrary to his rules of the game.

The value of land in the Permian Basin is an impossible commodity to appraise. Sales are as rare as unicorns in the land of scrub mesquite, Russian thistles and pump jacks. The highest and best use of the surface is as right of way and some takings rate favorably with square foot valuations in downtown Dallas.

"We'll take it," Goose said. "Now come on outside and I'll show you how good a shape my racing turtle is in."

Rocket was even more obedient to the tap of the coat hanger. As a matter of fact, Goose had to stop him from leaving the area completely. No longer did Rocket sputter, stop and pull in his running gear. Goose was obliged to arrest his flight and he did so after Rocket had traveled a full ten yards.

"That sucker can mobile can't he?" Goose giggled as he hoisted the turtle from the ground. The little legs were still churning and Rocket craned his neck around to stare at Goose.

Before Ben got away he and Goose agreed on Chris Finn's office in Merrit for the actual signing of the easement forms. Goose assured Ben that he, Cruickshank Jones, Simon Pleska and Frances Holiman would gather there. "You just be sure to show up with your checkbook," Goose said. "And I'm holding you to your agreement to drive me and Rocket over to Brisco for the turtle race. You've got a day off coming for buying all this here right of way!"

"I'll pick the instruments up before the week's out," Ben said. "Me and old Chris will go over them, count the structures on each place and I'll leave your money. In the meantime, I'd like to give the "go-ahead" to the surveying crew so that they can start the ground survey and make sure we don't hit any pipelines or put a tower in the middle of a lease road or a cow pen. Do you think that will be O.K.?"

"You bet," Goose said." I'll get aholt of everybody and as soon as Finn sets a time we'll be there. We can shake on that." He extended his right hand and Ben grasped it. The right of way was bought.

"You be sure and tell them surveyors to mind their manners when they're on Miss Holiman's section. She'd throw a wall eyed fit if they was to harm one of her animals. I figure she's still got that ten gauge scatter gun!"

"Wouldn't surprise me." Ben said.

chapter XXVII

"Come on in," Ben said, "the door's open. A look at his watch pleased him. Ben admired punctuality. He'd been a lot more dependable when he was younger. Kent was young and his arrival five minutes early was assurance that Ben had made a wise choice, for his second in command.

"Are we still eating at the cafeteria?" Kent asked.

"We'll eat anywhere you say. I most always eat at Furr's, so I can pick what I want, and don't have to wait for service, but whatever you want is available here in Vast Plain. I'll let you name your poison."

"Cafeteria's fine for me."

"Good, let's get on out there before there's a line. I don't much like to stand in line."

As they ate Kent reported the progress of the survey permission. He had five tracts, Hal had seven, Bob had eleven and Bill had two. J. J. was still familiarizing himself with the route on his section, but said that he'd about formulated his plans.

"Do they report to you regular?" Ben asked.

"Most ever night," Kent said. "I feel sort of funny about that, but they all know that you're running the show."

"You're running the show Kent. It's been so long since I've worked with anybody I've forgotten how to do it. The idea of having you guys report to me was not mine, so I've promoted you to acting Corporal on this project. You work with me, and they work for you.

"I've got several jobs on the line already and never know where I might be tomorrow. I talked this deal over with Brad and he gave his blessing. He told me to run it to suit myself, and that's what I'll do. After this line you won't be working as a middleman. Those who can do it don't need a boss and those who can't will be in a different line of work. I've seen a dozen come in and then decide that this job is not for them. I wouldn't be surprised if we lose a man or two on this part of the job."

"I didn't volunteer to buy right of way," Kent smiled, "and neither did any of the others. We weren't exactly threatened with losing our jobs, but places to go were few and far between. Bill Clemons was demoted to flunky when they closed his local office. He told me all about it. He's working his tail off, and has been out amongst them until way after sundown. So have the rest of us. Have you started on your permits?"

"I've got some back at the room that I'll turn over to you if we don't forget. Whoever is going in this weekend can drop them off at the office, or else you can collect them and put them in the mail. With a little luck we'll have most of them within a month."

"You're not going home?" Kent asked.

"Probably," Ben said, "but I'm going to come over to the Remuda and spend Friday night. Two or three of my landowners live around there and I hope to pick them off Saturday, before I go home. Next week I'm probably going to be tied up on the line out at Badger. I need to talk to the survey crew before they get started."

Kent told Ben of his career at TLC and his experiences at customer service. He told about his wife Lilly and that she was a real estate saleslady. Their son was away at college and Lilly couldn't stay home all the time, so she'd found work and really enjoyed it. They had a five acre place in the suburbs, chickens, a horse and a garden. Another ten years and their place would be paid for, according to Kent.

"I plan to take early retirement at fifty five. Lilly and I are going to buy a motor home and travel—at least that's our plan now."

"I hear you," Ben smiled. "me'n old Flossie have talked about the same thing, and I turn fifty five next January. My age and years with the company qualify me to try my hand at something else and if nothing slips, tears or breaks you'll be getting post cards from me saying 'I wish you were here.' Our daughter graduates high school next month and she's won a full music scholarship at TCU. Tuition, room and board all the way through, so we won't feel bad about letting her try her wings."

"Brad don't think you'll leave early. He told us that you enjoyed this work so much he couldn't run you off."

"As far as I'm concerned, I've got the best job in the world," Ben said. "I work when I need to and go home when I can. Nobody tallies my hours and I don't work in an office from eight to five. I wouldn't last a month in that damn office. I don't even go by there unless I have to. And I don't have to very often. I leave them alone and they leave me alone, and we live happily ever after."

"One thing bothers me a little bit," Kent said, "and it's got nothing to do with the job. It's something that happened last week when we were in the office."

"What's that?"

"You remember Harold Ackers. He came out of customer service with me and old Bob. Did you know he drums in a band?"

"Yeah, I heard that," Ben said, "can't remember who told me—maybe he did. He ain't married is he?"

"Has been, but not now. He's a good old boy, and has kept his music separated from his work. He told me he'll do the same thing now that he's a right of way buyer, so it's not so much that I'm worried about him. I'm a little concerned with that lady who works in the office. Ruby Jean Carter. She is married ain't she?"

"As far as I know," Ben said, "and she's got a kid—daughter I think. Why do you ask?"

"She showed up at the Sportsman where Hal's band was playing last Saturday night. Hal said she was by herself."

"That is kind of funny I guess," Ben admitted. "I've heard her say that she likes country music, so maybe she just wanted to hear Hal's band. She'll be our contact with the office, so I guess she wants to learn what she can about you new men. Did it bother Hal that she came out to hear him play?"

"No I don't think so. He invited her. What surprised him was her coming by herself. He said her table was right down front, and that he sat with her between sets. He said she was the best looking woman in the place. She wasn't wearing her work clothes, according to Hal."

"Well," Ben said, "I don't know what to make of it, but Harold and Mrs. Carter are both grown people and what they do off the job is nobody's business but theirs. Ruby is a good secretary and she's always been able to handle our appointments and act as our eyes and ears down at the throne room. What did Hal say about her showing up to see his band?"

"Not too much. But he was mighty surprised that her husband wasn't with her—I can tell you that!"

"I don't know that I've ever seen her husband," Ben admitted. "Maybe he don't like country music."

Kent left around nine o'clock, and agreed to reserve a room at the Remuda for Ben on Friday night. He also said that he would go home on Saturday.

"Everbody is going home Friday night except for you, me and Hal," Kent said. "Maybe we can have breakfast Saturday morning."

"I don't see why not," Ben agreed. "I've got three people to see and I'm going to the house. My daughter Donna has some kind of band performance Saturday night and I promised her I'd be there. I'll see you Saturday morning before you take off."

Chapter XXVIII

"Good morning councilor," Ben was ushered into Christopher Finn's office. "How is the world treating you?"

"Fine, fine!," Finn half rose and shook hands. "How's the land stealing pride of the electric industry?"

Several years ago Christopher Finn had been a major enemy of TLC and had single handedly forced them to raise their payment rate from five dollars per pole to twice that for distribution and service lines of voltages less than 125KV. He and Lyndon Moon had faced each other many times in condemnation hearings in Kismet County during those days and TLC had always come out on the losing side.

Eminent Domain is an expensive, method of acquiring right of way, and no way to make friends. Suits and appeals gets ink in area newspapers and Lyndon Moon grew weary of losing cases and money in those confrontations. The party that profited most, of course, was Christopher Finn.

Eventually TLC changed their method of payment on single pole lines. They were now negotiated just as transmission lines had always been.

Another condition Finn had imposed was the designation of a single representative of TLC. Ben had been agreed upon by both parties and was a familiar figure at Finn's office. Anytime a transmission or distribution line easement was negotiated successfully Ben drove three hundred miles from the home office, if necessary, to accept delivery and make payment. The distribution agents did not like the General Office hot shot handling any part in their business, but they could do nothing about it, so they swallowed their pride and waited helplessly for their easements to arrive by mail from the law office of Christopher Finn. Ben didn't like it either, but he was powerless to do anything about it. He did not however, publicize his feelings to anyone—especially the distribution right of way agents. "It's just part of my job" was about the only thing he'd ever said of the arrangement.

"I've got your easement from the Kelly Estate, the Simon Pleska Ranch and Cruickshank Jones, all executed and ready for filing. They've all been altered from your standard form just like the last ones. You write me the checks and I'll hand you the easements." Ben had his checkbook in his back pocket and he fished it out and set about his work.

"Consideration is seven hundred bucks a structure," Ben said as he wrote." At five structures to the mile, Mr. Kelly gets forty nine thousand, Mr. Jones gets seventeen five, Mr. Pleska has two miles which comes to seven thousand even, and Miss Holiman has thirty five hundred coming for her mile. Is that the way you've got it figured?"

"That's exactly right, but it ain't near enough money to suit me. You skinned all of them, but Kelly agreed. We get more than that for surface pipe lines."

"Mr. Kelly wants to see this country grow," Ben said as he wrote. "He don't want to stand in the way of progress. Neither do Mr. Jones, Mr. Pleska or Frances Holiman. By the way, did Miss Holiman sign her easement?"

"I don't know," Christopher smiled, "she took it home with her. She wants you to come by and pick it up. I guess she took a shine to you, or else she wants a check in her hand before she turns loose of that easement. I told her you'd come by."

"I can do that," Ben said. "Have you been out to her place?"

"You mean zoo don't you? Somebody gave her a kangaroo since you've been there. No. that's wrong—it's a wallaby—a pygmy kangaroo I guess. I'll bet she wants you to see her new baby."

"Maybe," Ben said as he pushed the three checks across the desk. "I can hardly wait." Christopher Finn put the executed easements into a legal size manila envelope and slid them to Ben. Their business completed, Christopher had his secretary bring coffee and they sat and made conversation until the cups were drained. Ben turned down a warm up.

"I've got to go and get my other easement," he said. "We need to go to work and Brad Hare won't go on the ground until he sees the signed easement. I'll have them let you know volume and page once they're recorded."

"I understand. Be careful not to run over any livestock out at the Holiman place. I'd hate to have you in court for running over a wallaby," Christopher Finn laughed out loud and walked to the front door with Ben.

An hour later Ben rolled cautiously up to Miss Holiman's residence. The area teemed with all manner of beast and fowl. Ben noticed that the wash pot was back on its legs. He wondered if Samantha had made it out alive. He sat in his car and waited patiently for Miss Holiman. He felt sure that she'd hear the din of the guinea flock that had gathered.

She descended her ramp and the big yellow dog followed closely behind her. Ben did not get out of the car until she neared and recognized him.

"Get out Mr. Drill," she took her customary seat and the dog curled up at her feet. She was not carrying a pitchfork this time as Ben joined her in the shade.

"How is Samantha," Ben asked. "I notice she's out of confinement."

"She's doing very well thank you, and she is reformed. Her hostility toward the rest of the children has completely vanished."

"I came to pick up my easement and pay you Miss Holiman. Your attorney sent me."

"Yes, I know. I'll go into the house and get it directly. First though I want to talk to you Mr. Drill."

"Yes ma'am. Do you have a question about the line construction?"

"No that procedure was explained in detail by Mr. Kelly and Mr. Finn. I understand the terms completely and have no problems with that. I want to talk to you on a personal matter. I mean no offense in what I'm about to tell you and there is no way I can explain how I know certain things. If at any time you feel uncomfortable or object to my frankness I will stop and let you go your way."

"Go ahead," Ben said, since he did not know what else to say. "First off though Miss Holiman I feel that I should tell you that I'm a married man."

"That is precisely what I want to address Mr. Drill. I too am united in spirit to Corporal Oliver Knight. The authorities reported his death on D Day, but he still calls on me from time to time, so you can see that a terrible mistake was made."

"Well, yes ma'am," Ben squirmed on his seat. "I guess I can see that."

"You cannot possibly understand," Miss Holiman smiled. "I don't ask you to understand. I just ask that you accept."

"O.K."

"Your wife was born in mid January in 1935," she began, "and you are five years older than she. The two of you have a daughter who is nearing adulthood.

"Both of you work and are in good health, but you need to quit smoking Raleigh cigarettes. She also needs to quit. Your teenage daughter is running around with that wild boy and he gives her cigarettes. You need to break them up at the earliest moment you can do so."

"How on earth did you find all that out?" Ben almost reached for a smoke. He caught himself just in time.

"I did not find it out. It came to me. I don't expect you to understand, but I'll go on if you're willing to listen."

"Go on."

"You must end your affair with that young red haired woman! Her husband knows she's seeing someone else and he is a jealous and dangerous person. Do not let her into your room again under any circumstances. It would be a tragic mistake!" she rose and motioned for Ben to follow. Wordlessly he fell in line behind her and the dog. In all his years Ben had never before been so stricken with wonder.

"You wait here. I don't allow anyone in my home, but I'll bring the easement to you. The dog lay down at the bottom of the inclined ramp and Miss Holiman scaled it on hands and knees. She vanished through the tapaulin drape. Ben looked out toward the tank and saw the wallaby nibbling a green tuft of grass.

Ben wrote Miss Holiman's check on the hood of his car as she and the dog stood and patiently waited for him to finish. His hands shook in the preparation, but he managed to get it done.

"Here you go Miss Holiman," he said as he extended his arm and gave her the check. Their hands touched and Ben sensed an electric shock. He released the check with an intake of breath and backed toward his car.

"Thank you Miss Holiman," Ben managed once he was inside with the door closed, "I appreciate your cooperation and everthing."

"You come and see me again," she said. "When your surveyors finish their job you must come and tell me before the construction crew arrives. And, be very careful in El Paso."

"I'll do that," Ben said as he backed up and drove slowly away.

"I'm not going to El Paso," Ben said to himself. "I think I've gone crazy instead."

Ben's only stop was at the Kelly place, but there was no one home. He drove to Vast Plain bought a six-pack and retreated to the comforting confines of his motel room. He locked and bolted the door.

chapter XXIX

"Have I got a place to sleep tonight?"

"Sure do, Mr. Drill. Got you all fixed up." Dawn slid his key across the desk. "How long will you be here?"

"Just tonight," Ben said. He didn't see Kent's car in the parking lot and didn't know Hal's vehicle so he bought a Saint Aaron newspaper and went to his room. "Both of 'em are working late," he thought aloud. He went inside, pulled his boots off stacked the pillows and lay down to work the crossword, while the TV droned across the room. As usual, he went sound asleep.

A knock on the door awakened Ben from his sleep. At first it was a "rap rap" but by the time he was fully awake the intensity and volume had increased enough to be heard several rooms away. A glance at his watch showed it was past eleven.

"I'm coming. I'm coming!" Ben said as he made his way to the locked door. "Hold your horses! I'm coming!"

He expected to see Kent, but Kent was not the man hammering on that door at eleven o'clock. Instead a young man, unknown to Ben, stood there and it was obvious that he was disturbed. He was looking into the interior of the room with an intensity that made Ben edgy.

"Are you Ben Drill?"

"Yes I am. Who are you?"

"My name is Don Carter!"

"I don't believe we've ever met," Ben brushed his hair back from over his eyes. "Are you sure you have the right room?"

"My wife Ruby works at your office in Metroplex. You don't know me, but I believe my wife is in your damn room, and if she is you and me are going to have a big problem!"

"There's nobody but me in this room," Ben backed up a step, "come on in and look for yourself." Don entered as Ben switched on the overhead lights and turned the television off. Don went into the bathroom, turned on the lights and then came back and peered under both beds.

"Looks like I owe you an apology Mr. Drill. I've just heard your name so many times I thought you might be the one messing around with my wife. I didn't know how old you were or anything. I might should have known better. You're not even a musician are you?"

"Nope" Ben admitted as he lit a cigarette, "just a hand at the light company—that's about it. You scared the hell out of me storming in here. What makes you think your wife is in Chalk Draw? You two live in Metroplex, don't you?"

"Yeah," Don sat down and asked for a smoke. Ben shook one out and fired up his lighter. Don drew in and began gasping, "goddamn, this cigarette ain't got no filter! I didn't know they still made them."

"One will satisfy you for a good while if you ain't used to them." Ben sat down on the edge of the bed.

"Ruby pulled out right after five. She said she was going to Midway to see her sick aunt. She's been going out there a lot lately and I've got reasons to believe that she's messing around on me again. After she was gone I found a book of matches from this motel. I got my mom to keep Chrissie and decided I'd do a little investigation. When I got off the Interstate and looked around this parking lot do you know what I found?"

"My room?"

"Nope—her car. It's parked out by the swimming pool. I went to the office and she's not registered—but you are! I put two and two together and thought I had you two caught! Made me madder than hell."

"I talk to Ruby three or four times a week," Ben admitted. "I tell her where I'll be, since I move around a lot. She knew I'd be here tonight. Just like she knew I was in Vast Plain last night. I wouldn't know her car if it run over me, but I know her and I've not seen her since I was in the office a couple of weeks ago."

"I can't figure out why her car's parked here," Don shook his head, "unless she's got another honey on the string."

"Maybe she had car trouble or something," Ben offered. "Is there someone over at Midway that could have come and picked her up?"

"Yeah, her sorry Uncle Avery could have," Don said. "But it looks like she should have called me."

"You might have already been on the road," Ben speculated. "It's a three hour drive to get here."

"That could be. I hadn't even thought of that. Since I'm this far though I'm going on and check it out. How far is it to Midway?"

"A little less than a hundred. You can make it in a couple of hours."

"I apologize again for rousting you out Mr. Drill. I should have known better, but I didn't know how old you are, and I didn't know whether you meddled in country music. If I'm not being too nosy, how old are you?"

"I'm fifty four. Your wife is probably young enough to be my daughter. Since I'm wide awake, would you like to have a cup of coffee before you hit the road for Midway?"

"Sounds great, but the restaurant is closed for the night."

"There's a truck stop a mile west of here," Ben said. "I'll comb my hair, put on my boots and meet you there in ten minutes. I went to sleep with my clothes on so I won't have to look for them." As the door closed behind Don, Ben lit another cigarette and found his boots. Frances Holiman was one in a million.

Ben bought the coffee and wished Don well as he backed away from the truck stop. Don started to apologize again, but Ben stopped him. "Don't apologize Don. Hell, when a man's wondering where his wife is and what she's up to he'll do crazy things. I hope everything works out for you two. Be careful when you go through Dry Lake. They've usually got at least two speed traps set up over there, so hold your speed around the limit."

Back in his room Ben dialed Kent's room. He responded on the third ring. Ben identified himself as Kent roused and tried to get his bearings. He was still not used to sleeping away from home, where the phone was on Lily's side of the bed.

"Wake up and get your britches on Kent. I need to come over and talk to you. It's important or I wouldn't wake you up."

"Give me a minute!"

Briefly Ben told of his visitor, and the reason for the call. Kent sat on his bedside and listened with keen interest. He lit a smoke and located an ashtray.

"Well, you can see she ain't here, if that's what you thought. And I haven't seen her!"

"That's not what I thought Kent. Is Harold still registered here? That's what I need to know. If by some chance she's with him we need to do something. Ruby's husband may be back this way before the night's out."

"He moved across the Interstate to the Holiday yesterday."

"How come?"

"They've got a little club over there," Kent said. "Hal said he was going to spend a couple of nights there and check it out. He thought he might get a booking for that band he plays with."

"Do you remember telling me about Ruby showing up at that place in Metroplex? It would be one hell of a note if she came out here for an encore. I know Hal ain't married, but she is. If she's over there they both need to know."

"I'll run over there right quick," Kent found his shirt.

"No, don't do that. If she's in his room you don't want to catch them. A phone call would be lots better."

"I'll bet you're right Ben. Where's that phone book?"

"Top dresser drawer," Ben said, and that's where it was.

"I want you to leave me out of this Kent. Hal don't even need to know that Don came to my room. Let's let him think that the night clerk may have alerted you. Just tell him what happened. Don't even ask if she's there. If she's not, then the only harm done is he got woke up. If she is, let them work out their own arrangements."

"How come that guy come to this motel and woke you up anyway?" Kent asked with a little suspicion.

"Her car is parked out by the swimming pool, and mine was the only name he knew associated with TLC," Ben said. "He said he'd heard Ruby talk about me."

Kent walked to the front window and parted a couple of slats. Ben rose and looked out with him. There was only one car near the pool.

"Hal," Kent said, "I apologize for waking you up at this hour of the night, but it's sort of an emergency."

"Emergency—what kind? Is the world ending?" Hal asked.

"Nope, but Ruby's husband Don was here. He says he spotted her car in our parking lot. He thinks it may have broke down I guess. I couldn't tell him anything except that I haven't seen her. According to him she was on her way to Midway, and that maybe someone came over here to pick her up. He left a little bit ago to go on to Midway, so if you happen to see her you might let her know."

"Are you talking about the Ruby in our office?"

"Yep, her husband's looking for her, and he's damn mad!"

"Maybe, he'll find her over at Midway."

"O. K., I'll see you tomorrow. Sorry I had to disturb you"

"Good job Kent, now turn out the lights, look out and see what happens," Ben said.

Within ten minutes, Hal's car pulled up beside the car at the pool. With little wasted motion Ruby unlocked the doors and Hal deposited her suitcase and clothing in the back seat. The car backed out, and Ruby was on her way.

Hal watched her go, and looked toward Kent's darkened room. Then he drove away.

"Did you see anything Kent?"

"Nope, I went right back to bed after I called. You see anything?"

"How could I? I'm not even here."

chapter xxx

"Dad, a man called for you this morning. He said it was important. I wrote his phone number down on that envelope by the phone."

"Thanks Donna," Ben said as he put his dirty clothes on a chair. "Where'd you say. O.K., here it is, but you didn't get his name. Do you remember it?"

"No, I was having a hard time getting his phone number right because I couldn't find a pencil. Then I forgot his name. They'll tell you when you call that number," Donna was teasing Pedro by spraying him with the ironing mister. Pedro would growl fiercely and attack her shoes.

Ben dialed the number, but Donna had made an error when she recorded it. The voice was that of a Spanish-speaking lady who was suspicious of crank calls. When he identified himself she hung up. "If it's really important he'll call back I guess." He threw the number in the wastebasket. "I don't want to talk to anybody anyhow."

Donna said that she'd broken up with Derek, and would never date again. Ben, of course was glad to hear the news, but he squelched his elation and offered his sympathy at her disappointment and heartbreak.

"When's graduation?"

"Two weeks from yesterday. May 31st at 8 P.M. to be exact! Are you going to be home?"

"Wild horses couldn't keep me away," Ben said. "It's not every day that I have a daughter graduate from high school. With a full college scholarship and an 'A' average. I'll be there!"

Flossie came in at noon—she only worked a half-day on Saturday, and she and Donna got the catalogs out to plan a wardrobe for college. She gave Ben a quick kiss to the cheek.

"You need a shave," she said.

"Didn't shave this morning. I found two landowners and headed for the house. How about we have supper over at Four Winds. It's been a good while since we've been there. Would you like to go with us Donna?"

"I guess so. Unless I get a better offer."

The phone rang and Donna answered on the first ring. It was not whoever she was expecting and her disappointment was evident on her face. "It's for you dad," she said as she covered the mouthpiece. "I think it's the man who called earlier." Ben sighed at the prospect that something had gone awry somewhere—miles away probably.

"Yes sir," he said, "how can I help you?"

"J. J. Tolliver here. I hate to bother you on your day off, but I really need to talk to you if you've got time."

"You bet, time's all I've got. What do you have on your mind?"

"I'd like to meet you someplace where we can talk privately and face to face." J. J. said. "I'll drive down to Bo Dark and meet you any place you say if you can spare a few minutes. It's an important matter, and you're the only one I know who can help me."

"Do you know where the Hwy. Robery Cafe is?"

"No, but I can find it. Bo Dark's not all that big. What time will be convenient for you? I can be there in thirty minutes."

"I'll meet you there in thirty minutes then," Ben said.

J. J. arrived in twenty eight minutes. Ben was already nursing a cup of coffee, and waved for J. J.'s attention as he came in the door.

J. J. seated himself nervously, and waited for the waitress to bring his coffee before he spoke. He looked like he'd been missing out on his sleep.

"Mr. Drill," he said, "I don't think I can handle this job, and I don't know what to do about it. I didn't get permission on any of my tracts last week. Kent don't know it. I didn't think it was his business to know. Brad Hare told me that you were the lead man, so I waited to talk to you."

"Don't call me Mr. Drill J. J.," Ben smiled. "It makes me feel old. What gave you trouble last week? Maybe I can help."

The landowners J. J. had contacted had been the problem. The first three he'd seen had informed him that the oil companies compensated landowners before they entered for surveys. That way, the owners knew that they'd get their money. TLC was the only company who wanted to wait until the job was done, and it didn't make sense. What if they abandoned a route and didn't come back? J. J. didn't know what to say in response.

"Most land owners don't grant survey permission or sell right of way to TLC," Ben said. "They sell it to you and it's up to you to convince them that you'll be back no matter what. We've never paid first and asked an owner to sign a release. It's to his advantage to wait. If somebody leaves a gate open or catches the pasture on fire with a cigarette we mean to pay what is fair to make it right. That's why we wait. I thought you knew that."

"I did, and that's what I told them, but they didn't believe me. Two of them said that all land agents were liars. They made me feel like a beggar, and I couldn't get them to sign. I've decided that I'm not going to be able to do this job, if I can't pay what they're getting from other companies. I told them I wouldn't want to wait either."

"I wish you hadn't told them that," Ben said. "Even if that's the way you feel. You should have kept it to yourself. Put yourself in their place and see how it sounds."

"That's what my wife told me too," J. J. admitted, "but what's done is done. I just don't think I can handle this line of work. Is there anything else I could try? If not, I guess I'll be without a job unless I can find a place in another department." J. J. sipped his coffee and his worry was etched deeply in his brow. "I'm sorry, but that's the way I feel. I'm ready to give up." Despite his dislike for J. J. Tolliver, Ben could not help a feeling of sympathy. He lit a cigarette as the waitress refilled his cup.

"I'll tell you what J. J.," he said after a long and thoughtful silence, "there may be another way for you to get some experience and stay in the right of way business. I can't promise, but I've got something for you to think about. I'll go to bat for you if you're willing to try."

"I'll try anything—except getting survey permission."

Ben explained the two construction projects underway—one between Willow Park and High Bank and another from Gruver to Whitlow. Construction was being done by Moore Construction on both lines and a TLC inspector was assigned to each operation. His role was to monitor and make sure that the line was built to company specifications. In the past, when the workload allowed, a right of way agent had also accompanied the erection crew to be sure that the rights of both landowner and TLC were protected. It was, by nature, not an extremely demanding responsibility for the agent, but his presence and availability was a comfort to the landowner. His role was that of troubleshooter and peacemaker. Ben told him of his recent trips to construction sites, and what he'd done to try and keep the job running smoothly and on schedule. With an agent on hand during the actual construction, crop loss and any other damage can be cataloged on a daily basis and such information is valuable when the job is completed.

"Do you think you could give me a chance at that?" J. J. asked. "Would I still be a right of way agent?"

"You let me handle it," Ben said. "Which line do you think you'd be interested in?"

"How about the one to High Bank? How long is it and what is its stage of completion?"

"I can't tell you exactly J. J., but it's about a hundred road miles and I'd say the job is around the half way mark. Most of the tracts are pasture, with some grain and cotton where they'll lose a strip of their crop. With you along, we'll have a good basis for calculating how much loss they suffer and that will be a big help when we pay damages. Since Brown, Gankle and I bought that line there's going to be someone different coming around when the job's done anyway. You could let the folks along the line that you'll be the one making the last call. When it's time to pay damages you'll be the man with the checkbook, and the landowner will be more of a beggar than you. Kinda like horse trading, but you'll decide what's fair when all the evidence is in. You won't be asking—you'll be the man in charge!"

"I'd really like to try it," J. J. said eagerly. "Will anybody on the construction job be my boss?"

"Nope, and you're not their boss either. You're along strictly as a representative of right of way."

"When will you let me know something?" J. J. asked as he drained his coffee.

"At our get together in Chalk Draw Monday morning. This coffee's my treat. You can rest easy and don't worry. I should have already put a man with the construction bunch now that I think about it. But I still want you to show up in Chalk Draw so we can decide how to split up your paperwork on that job."

"I really appreciate this Ben, and I'll not disappoint you."

"If you satisfy the company it will tickle me plumb to death. See you on Monday. Have a good weekend and don't worry."

Back home Ben called Brad Hare and told him what had happened and what he had in mind.

"What you decide is your business Ben. I just want the land I need. You get the right of way and I'll build the lines."

"Thanks, that's the way I figured it too, and I appreciate your not calling me when you have trouble designing a tower."

chapter XXXI

They grouped at the round table and everyone was drinking coffee by eight—even Bill. He'd not missed his exit ramp and was proud of his accomplishment. Even the waitress complimented him.

"I always put the cart before the horse", Ben began, "but now I'm going to try and get off at the right ramp like old Bill did." Everyone smiled and Bill laughed aloud.

"I'm not wearing a suit and tie this time," Bill said. "Florence let me leave them at home, and she bought me a pair of boots too. They'll keep the grass burrs out of my socks. I learned things last week, and got survey permission on eleven of my tracts."

"Sounds like you had a good week Bill. A damn good one for the first week!" The others agreed.

"You'll have more to pick from when I tell you of our revised battle plan," Ben said. "I'm going to ask J. J. to turn in his portion of the permission sheets. He's going to pull off this job and ride herd on construction of the Willow Park—High Bank 138KV line. The construction people have a representative on that job. Sam Dolan is their man, and he observes the tower erection and the sagging of the conductor. His job is making sure the contractor does his job.

"Before we ran out of agents, we kept a man on new construction too, but we haven't been able to do that since our agents thinned out. I've already discussed this with J. J. and he's willing to take the job on."

"I'm going to miss the fellowship and coffee on Mondays," J. J. said, "but Ben has convinced me that I'm needed at another location, and I'm ready and willing to go. Luckily, I did not secure a single permission last week, but I do have a spiral notebook with information that will help to locate forty-six of my clients quickly. I, of course, will donate the accumulated information to the cause. I have all my paper work in the car."

"There's also a 345KV line under construction from Gruver to Whitlow," Ben said, "and if one of you would like to go south you could watch that line going up. Do I have a volunteer?"

"I'd like to do it," Bob said. "That's farming country and I was raised on a dirt farm in Oklahoma. I had several courses in FFA figuring cotton and grain yields and know some about farming. But, if anyone else wants to volunteer, I'll stay on this job. I secured twenty six of mine last week, and enjoyed the work."

"Anybody else want the job," Ben asked. "We can draw straws if we need to." Hal, Bill and Kent agreed that Bob should go. They said they wanted to continue the job they were on.

"O.K." Ben said. "It's a done deal—let's have breakfast and put J. J. and Bob on the road. Then we'll divvy up their tracts. And let me remind you all to let Ruby know where you're staying in case Brad or somebody needs to get hold of you." Ben couldn't help notice that Hal blushed, but he did not look up from his coffee.

They went to Kent's room with the paper work they'd collected and agreed that Kent would divide it up when he had time. Nobody needed any more clients to stay busy for the upcoming week.

"Hal, do you already have a room here in Chalk Draw," Kent asked.

"No."

"Maybe you'd be better located if you went back to Blessing. That way we'll be spaced out about right, for the time being at least."

"Suits me," Hal said. "I got eight or ten tracts last week, and most of them are on the west end. It will be just as handy to headquarter in Blessing."

"Bill will still be in Groom, you'll be in Blessing, I'll stay here at Chalk Draw and Ben will be at Midway or Vast Plain at the west end. That's not bad spacing and with me in the middle we can all meet here next week and split up what J. J. and Bob turned back. That sound okay Ben?"

"Suit's me," Ben said, "and I'll be at Ramada Inn over at Vast Plain. I've still got a few things to do on my line out west."

"I'll put my stuff in the room then," Kent said, "and we'll meet here next Monday." Bill and Hal drove away to the east and Ben asked Kent if he'd like one more coffee before he went to work.

"I thought you'd never ask—who's buying?"

"You are," Ben said.

"When did you decide all this?" Kent asked once they were seated and each had a cigarette going.

"Over the weekend. I talked it over with Brad and he didn't have any objections. With those guys looking out for our side while they're putting those lines in the air, we won't be pulled off our project and jerked from one end of the system to the other."

"J. J. couldn't get the job done, could he?"

"He didn't turn in any permission forms did he?"

"Nope." Kent said.

"Did you happen to talk to Hal this weekend?" Ben asked. "I'm not trying to pry into his business, and I'll never mention Friday night, but I'm curious to know how everything turned out."

"He called me at home on Sunday," Kent admitted. "He said Ruby showed up at the night club again, and by herself. So I guess everything went O.K. for everybody. Hal said she didn't have any black eyes or bruises. Neither does he."

"I'm glad, and I hope he profited from the experience. I guess there's a lesson there for all of us."

"The moral," Kent said, "is don't mess around with married women with big jealous husbands."

"Especially if that married lady works the same place you do," Ben agreed. "The only thing that could make it more chancy would be if Hal was married too."

"He was in a spot I wouldn't want to be in. I'll tell you that for sure?"

"Me either Kent. I'm going to Vast Plain. Good hunting—and I'll see you next Monday."

Ben tuned in KJBC and sang along with Merle Haggard on "Mama Tried." It was going to be a good week. The sun was warm, the wind was not blowing, and the great turtle race was next Saturday.

The next selection was Wynn Stewart doing "It's Such a Pretty World."

chapter XXXII

Ben arrived at the Kelly place around sun up, just as he'd promised, and Goose was cleaned up and ready to go. He sported a shined pair of boots and an ironed shirt for the occasion.

"Man alive," Ben said, "you're all duded up! I hope you ain't disappointed with the way I look. My old boots look bad next to your new kicks."

"They might want to take a picture of me getting that new pickup," Goose smiled. "I want to look spiffy when old Baird hands over them keys."

"How's Rocket? Is he set to run a hundred yard dash?"

"He's hot to trot," Goose said. "We've been training two or three hours a day for the last week, and he's the fastest one I ever trained. Them other entries won't see nothing but his back side."

"Well, I cleaned out the inside of the car so we'll both have a place to sit and we can put Rocket in the floorboard where he'll be comfortable."

"I've got him a bushel basket," Goose said. "Got some rags in the bottom in case he springs a leak or something. Don't want to mess up your car."

"He won't mess up that car Mr. Kelly. It's already a mess."

"Mr. Drill, I want you to quit calling me Mr. when we get over to the race track. Call me Goose like everybody else does. I'd like them to think that we're lifetime compadres, so they'll be willing to hustle you for a few bets. There's money to be made and I mean to bankroll you. We'll both come out on the long end. Me with a new pickup and you with a pocket full of money. And from here on I mean to call you Ben."

"That suits me fine Goose." Ben wondered what Goose meant about bankrolling, but he didn't ask.

"We're ready to roll, Ben," Goose deposited his basket in the back floorboard. "Fame, fortune, a new pickup truck and riches await us at the race track." They were on the Interstate in ten minutes and westward bound.

"Will your wife be coming down to see the races Mr. Kelly? Goose, I mean."

"No, but I invited her. She said she couldn't leave town this weekend. I guess she had to work."

"I thought maybe I'd get to meet her," Ben said. "What grade does she teach?"

"Eighth, and she's been mighty busy this year. She's only been home twice since Christmas."

"That's the way me and my wife live," Ben said. "I'm always on the road and lucky to be home two weekends in a month. I live in motel rooms and Flossie spends her days working and seeing after our teenage daughter. It's a tough old row to hoe for all three of us. Not much like Ozzie and Harriet—that's for sure!"

"I met Wanda when I was up at Texas Tech," Goose said. "I tried college for a year, but I didn't much like it and couldn't make my grades. I had me an athletic scholarship. When I was young I could knock a baseball for half a mile. Wanda come to all my games. She was the prettiest girl in Lubbock and I don't mind telling you—I wanted that girl for my own. The way it turned out, she wanted me too—for my daddy's money, but I didn't know that back then."

Ben did not interrupt.

"I dropped out and come home, and she got to coming down to Minotaur on the bus to see me. We had a high old time while she went on through college and got her teaching degree. Daddy and momma liked her too and they bought her an Oldsmobile to go back and forth in. She didn't miss many weekends coming down here."

"Sounds like she thought a lot of you," Ben said. "It's a pretty long drive from here to Lubbock."

"It don't take long in an Oldsmobile Ninety Eight, Ben."

"How long have you two been married now Goose? Got any kids?"

"No kids. We've been married for twenty-two years last February. She's had that teaching job in El Paso for twenty of it. She could get a job at Minotaur, but she ain't happy out here on the ranch—and I ain't happy in El Paso. Too damn many people and cars. If I lived out there for a month I'd probably blow my brains out with a shotgun. If I didn't get run over first."

"That's the way I feel about the Metroplex," Ben said. "We live in

Bo Dark, eighty miles from my office, but I'd rather drive that eighty miles as live there."

"Wanda don't like Badger atall," Goose continued, "and she hates the ranch house. I told her I'd build her any house she wanted, but she turned me down. She did say that she might change her mind one of these days."

"I hope so Goose. Maybe she's working for that teacher retirement. I've heard it's pretty good."

"I hope you won't think I'm bragging Ben, but I've already got more money than you and me can count. It ain't the money. She's got a big old house in the silk stocking section of El Paso, a brand new town car and anything else she takes a mind to have. So, it couldn't be just for the money. I study about it sometimes, but I can't really figure out what she wants. Christopher says she married me for my money. I didn't believe him at first, but sometimes I think he might be right. He drew up some kind of prenuptial papers and got her to sign them. I don't know exactly what they say, but he tells me I've got a lot better protection than I deserve if me and Wanda was to split up. She probably knows the deal better than I do."

"Life does get complicated don't it?" Ben said. "Do you worry about her out there in El Paso?"

"Don't have to Ben. I've got a private detective on my payroll that don't have no other duty but to watch over her. Manuel Martines is his name and he's a good watchdog. She don't even know it, but he follows her to school and from school to home and even when she goes shopping. The only time she's out of his sight is when she goes to the bathroom or to bed. He's worked her case ever since she's been in El Paso. I pay him more to look after her than she draws from her job."

"And she don't even know?"

"Guess not. She's never mentioned it, and we talk on the phone most ever night."

"Man alive," said Ben. "Sounds like a Perry Mason deal!"

They got off the Interstate at the Barton exit and Goose directed Ben to the site of the International Championship of Racing Turtles. Goose reached into his boot top and handed Ben an inch thick bank deposit bag as they eased to a stop.

"There's ten thousand dollars in there," he said, "I want you slip it in your boot before we get out. The race don't start for another thirty minutes or so. While I'm putting my turtle through his paces at the staging area I want you to mingle around and see how much you can bet on my turtle winning. You'll most likely have to give odds. Hold off for an even bet for awhile and then offer two to one odds."

"I don't feel right about all this," Ben said. "What happens if your turtle don't win?"

"He'll win!" Goose said. "I always win. But if he breaks a leg or lightning strikes him and I lose it ain't going to cost you a dime. That's walking around money and if we throwed it in the Cielo Vista River, I wouldn't miss a meal. And neither will you." Reluctantly Ben slid the pouch into his boot leg and pulled his pants back over his boot top. Immediately he regretted not unzipping the bag to see for sure the money was there.

They got out and Goose picked his turtle from the basket. He drew hoots as soon as he was recognized.

"Here's ol' Goose! The nine time winner and his galloping terrapin!" someone greeted.

"Goose has gone and hired him a chauffeur," yelled another. There were probably a hundred men milling around the area, and they apparently all knew Goose.

At the staging area Ben stopped at the edge of a fifty-foot diameter circle of watered and packed sand. The circle was outlined with a precise line of chalk, and only contestants were allowed to walk across the racing surface. There were already seven box turtles positioned near the center of the oval. The owner's names were affixed to each of the contestants. A big K, apparently done with nail polish, was on Goose's entry. Some had strips of paper held in place with clear tape and one sported a small Texas flag secured by glue.

"You a friend of Goose?" someone asked.

"Yeah, I've known him all my life," Ben replied. "Who might you be?"

"Names Dirk, I'm from over in Roswell. That's my turtle with the Texas flag. I call him Maple Syrup."

"Maple Syrup?"

"Yeah, he runs slow in the winter but he's quick on his feet during the summer. This is his forth year and I believe he'll bring home the trophy. Matter of fact, I'd put money on him."

"Goose says he's got a good one too," Ben said. "But he says it ain't near as fast as last year's entry. Maybe we'll have a good race."

"Goose always says that," Dirk laughed. "He's been telling that same sad story for the past nine years, and he's won every blessed time. He didn't mention how he trains his turtles to you, did he?"

"He won't tell," Ben said. "I've asked him, but he won't say. For all I know, he can talk to turtles."

Silently the two stood and watched as Solomon Simpson of Alpine added his entry to the congregation in the circle. His entry was number nine. The start of the race was sheduled in fifteen minutes, and the crowd was still growing.

The racing oval was surrounded by a foot rise in elevation, which enabled the fans to look down and view the action, much like a minature football stadium..

Dirk introduced Ben to several more of the racing turtle owners. Goose was across the circle talking with people on that side. Ben looked at the vehicles that were parked haphazardly all around and it looked like a showroom for Lincoln, Cadillac and Mercedes. His was the cheapest vehicle in the collection. There was also a fire engine red Chevrolet pickup surrounded by pickets with a binder twine connecting them. Little banners of tape were fluttering from the cord.

"That's the prize that goes to any man who can win ten races," Dirk said. "Goose is the only one with a chance, since he's won nine in a row. Old man Baird would die of a stroke if Goose was to win, but I don't think it will happen. He'll be the favorite, but that don't mean he's going to win. Hell, I believe I can beat him. A New Mexico turtle is higher geared than Texas terrapins.

"Gentlemen, I'd like your attention," a tall and imposing man stood atop a raised platform of cinder blocks. Talk stopped and all attention was focused on the towering figure. "This here tortoise race will begin in ten minutes and I am here in an unofficial capacity to see that the contest is conducted fairly. I am Sheriff of this county and I will not condone overt gambling at this sporting event, so don't let me see any money change hands. If you wish to make friendly wagers, I will be blind and deaf to that, but payoffs will be made at a place that I cannot see. I suggest that these transactions be conducted to the north of that new pickup truck. I will be to the south of it. You are all welcome at this forty sixth International Turtle Race, and I hope you enjoy yourselves. Now I will go back to my vehicle and allow you gentlemen to inspect the twelve hardshell contestants and back your convictions with the national medium of exchange. When those negotiations are completed I will stand upon this altar of cinder blocks and fire the starting shot—and if you lose your wager I expect you to pay it. I would be disappointed if anyone does otherwise."

True to his word the sheriff walked to his vehicle, got in and sat down to allow ten minutes to tick away. Betting was brisk, but no actual cash emerged from any pocket. Just as Goose had predicted Ben had to give odds to get the money covered.

"One will get you two over here," he said. "I've got ten thousand dollars that says Goose Kelly's turtle will win. If you are of a different opinion I will gladly cover your bets up to a total of ten thousand dollars."

The odds fell on receptive ears and Ben's money was covered in five minutes.

The twelve owner/handlers walked to the center of the arena, the sheriff stepped back atop his blocks and fired a single shot from his service revolver.

Some pushed with their boot toes to urge their turtle to motion, others got down on hands and knees, while a couple whistled shrilly. Goose dropped small gravels on Rocket's shell and he immediately extended his head and little stubby legs and went into action. When he crossed the finish line his nearest competitor was six feet behind and three had not moved at all.

While Ben was stuffing hundred dollar bills into his shirt Goose picked up his turtle and made directly for Mr. Baird to claim the keys to his new pickup truck. The turtle was in one hand and the trophy was under that arm. Reluctantly, Mr. Baird dropped the keys into Goose's free hand and left the festivities immediately. The sheriff followed him closely and cooler boxes filled with canned beer were produced from many of the parked cars.

"Let's get out of here," Goose said. "When you get back to the Interstate turn west. Don't fool around and I'll meet you in Flat Land. Park behind the Ace Cafe." Ben did as he was told and watched Goose trailing him a half mile back. He parked at the rear of the Ace Cafe, and Goose pulled in beside him. He was all smiles when he opened the door and sat down with Ben.

"We come this way just to be on the safe side," Goose smiled. "I don't think we have anything to worry about, but even if somebody did get ideas they would figure we went east back over to the ranch. What did I tell you about that Rocket! Didn't he make them others look bad?"

"He really did" Ben said as he reached into his boot and retrieved Goose's money pouch. "man I'm glad to get that back in your hand. Now just wait a minute and I'll dig your winnings out. Hell, I stuffed it in my other boot, my pockets and my shirt. All five thousand!" Ben began to lay the wadded mass of money on the car seat.

"I believe that's all of it Goose," Ben said. "Do you want to count it?"

"That money belongs to you Ben. I got a brand new pickup out of the deal and a trophy. I've got all the money I need and I mean for you to keep the cash winnings. And, our friendship depends on you're saying 'thank you Goose.' Don't you go and disappoint me."

"Thank you Goose," Ben said, but he was not comfortable with the arrangement. He'd find a way to leave that money when they got back to the ranch house.

"Wad it up and put it in your glove box," Goose smiled. "Then come look my new pickup over and I'll buy you a cup of coffee."

chapter XXXIII

"Saturday is your day off ain't it Ben?" Goose and Ben were on their second warm up at the Ace Coffee Shop, and the only customers in the place. They'd discussed and re-discussed the turtle race and how Rocket had outclassed the other entries when Goose asked the question.

"Kind of my day off," Ben admitted, "unless I get called out on an emergency. Why do you ask?"

"I want you to go to El Paso with me Ben. I get mighty nervous in all that traffic, and I need to see Wanda. It ain't but a couple of hours on over there. I wouldn't ask if it wasn't real important. We could spend the night and have you home on Sunday." Goose obviously hated to ask the favor, but he asked it all the same.

"I don't know Goose," Ben said. "Let me call home before I give you an answer."

Donna answered the phone and Ben could tell that she'd been dozing. He could hear Pedro barking to protest the ring of the telephone. Flossie was not yet home from work and Ben assured Donna that he'd be home next Thursday for graduation ceremonies, but he'd have to stay in West Texas for the weekend.

"I'll be out of pocket tonight and Sunday morning," Ben said, "but you can leave a message for me at the Remuda in Chalk Draw if you need to. I should be back there by noon tomorrow and I'll call you and mom."

"O.K.," Donna said. "Shut up Pedro! I'll tell mom when she comes in. Your secretary called around nine o'clock this morning, but she didn't say what she needed. And, she didn't ask for you to return the call."

"I love you Donna, and don't worry. There's no way I'm going to miss your graduation. Hug mom for me. And thump Pedro on the nose—he'll quit barking."

"I know, then he'll bite me," Donna laughed. "Be careful—I love you too." Ben returned to the table.

"I can run you out to El Paso Goose but I need to be back in Chalk Draw by dinner time tomorrow. I'd like for us to go in my car. I'm used to driving it. Can we leave your pickup here?"

"Sure," Goose beamed. "Ace is an old buddy of mine and he owns this place."

On the long road to El Paso, Ben returned to the matter of the five thousand dollars in his glove box. He told Goose that he just didn't feel right about keeping any of that money. "You took the chance of losing ten thousand dollars Goose, so that money is rightly yours."

"Did you open that bank bag I handed you?" Goose asked.

"No."

"Then you don't know for a fact that I risked anything do you?"

"It was full of something," Ben said, "and I figure it was money."

"You didn't see it though, did you?"

"Well, no."

"Then we got nothing else to talk about. I overheard you telling your daughter that you'd be home for her graduation. Buy her a nice present with your winnings."

Ben was curious about the purpose of the mission and tried to find out without being obvious. He told Goose that he had made many trips to El Paso back in the sixties when he first became a member of the American Right of Way Association.

That organization had formed in California and had expanded to El Paso back then and had since swept across Texas, but in the beginning Ben had driven out to monthly meetings at the Cortez Hotel. The meetings were always followed by a trip across the Rio Grande to Jaurez.

"You mean to tell me you belong to a union? I didn't know you lease men were organized."

"Naw, we're not a union. But we do have a monthly get together," Ben said. "I've got a plaque that says I'm a Senior Right of Way Agent. I qualified because I'd been at it for enough years. Nowadays you've almost got to be a Philadelphia lawyer to get the certification. That's the way it goes in most organizations, seems like. In the beginning you don't need much more that a heartbeat to join, but then, first thing you know the standards are raised and there's a bar exam like the lawyers have. I'm already a dinosaur. An old wore out agent. Now, our organization is nationwide with disciplines, training courses and all the trimmings. I probably couldn't even qualify to join today."

As they began to see the outline of buildings and the smoke from industry on both sides of the Rio Grande, Goose decided to confess his compulsion to see Wanda. He suspected that she was up to something, but for the life of him, he couldn't figure out what.

"That damn detective calls in every Saturday night," Goose snorted, ""and says there's nothing to report. Wanda calls on Sunday and says there's nothing to report. A year ago they always had something to report, and it's damn funny to me that neither one of them has anything important to report! I aim to see for myself."

They arrived in El Paso as the sun was sinking behind the Franklin Mountains and Goose guided Ben to Wanda's residence. He didn't know street names, but he was unerring in his recognition of landmarks. "Off the Interstate at that Texaco station, left at the Piggly Wiggly and right at that stand of trees in the park," he directed and then he told Ben to pull over to the curb at the front of a house with a Realtor sign in the front yard. From that point Goose pointed out the house where Wanda lived. It could more aptly be described as a mansion in Ben's estimation. The most imposing structure in what appeared to be an ultra-high class neighborhood. Manicured lawns, flawless landscaping and top of the line vehicles parked in driveways was evidence that none of the houses were rented by the month.

"Man alive!" Ben said, "this looks like Beverly Hills."

"That house cost two hundred thousand," Goose said matter of factly. "We paid cash, and it's gone up since we bought it."

"Do you reckon the cops will think we're planning a robbery if they see us parked here?" Ben thought of the cash in his glove box. "Maybe I should stash that cash someplace else in case one stops and searches the car."

"I got a deputy badge from Draw County," Goose said. "We ain't going to have any trouble with the law. There ain't no lights on in the kitchen, but it ain't hardly six o'clock yet. She'll be coming home soon and she comes from the other direction. Wanda won't pay no attention to us being parked here." A glance at his watch told Ben that the time was five forty five.

Within ten minutes Goose's knowledge of Wanda's schedule proved to be accurate. A beige Lincoln Town Car pulled into the driveway and Wanda got out, but not from the driver's side. A man in a dress suit got out that door and preceded Wanda to the massive front door. He unlocked it, Wanda entered and he followed.

"That son of a bitch!" Goose said.

"Who is he?"

"Manuel Martines," Goose said," the detective I pay to watch over Wanda. And that's my car too!"

"Maybe he's just bringing her home," Ben said. "Somebody may be going to pick him up."

"Bullshit!" Goose said. "They're not even supposed to know each other." The lights came on in the house. "They're in the kitchen, and he's probably trying to call in his report to me that everything's fine. Let's get out of here Ben!"

"Where do you want to go?"

"I want to go somewhere and buy a gun."

"You can't do that Goose," Ben gasped. "Maybe we should just sit here awhile and keep our eyes open. You don't want to shoot anybody." They sat quietly for an hour and all the lights went out.

"Now, we'll go buy a gun," Goose said grimly.

"I believe you'd be making a bad mistake Goose. You need to go home and talk to your lawyer. If he made all those papers for your protection you need to know exactly what they say. Lawyers can hurt people a lot more than guns and you can't be jailed for possession or use of a lawyer."

"I guess you're right," Goose admitted, "but I'd sure like to gut shoot both of them!"

"Tell you what," Ben said, "the night's young and just across the Santa Fe Bridge, Juan Peso is emceeing adult entertainment. You and me need a little R and R, and a trip to Jaurez does more good than a session with a psychiatrist. I'll buy the margaritas."

"You're money ain't no good on this trip Ben. I'll go, but you ain't spending your money on me. You've done more already than a man could be expected to do."

Juan Peso greeted Ben warmly and asked why it had been so long between visits. Loud horns rendered bump and grind music as shapely girls writhed and wiggled on the dimly lighted stage.

"Father Time and Mother Nature has about taken all the starch out of me Juan," Ben said as a stripper danced her way from the stage and onto the ring side table top where he and Goose had been seated. Ben slapped her on the flank and she pouted and stepped back to the stage. They stayed until the wee hours and Goose got lit up on margaritas and a lot calmer. Ben paid for the drinks because he had an expense account and was entertaining a land owner.

Back at the Cortez they got a room with two beds and neither removed any apparel except their foot wear.

"I want to be back where I can see my front yard at seven in the morning," Goose said. Ben called the desk and arranged a six thirty wake up call.

They had an eye-opener cup of coffee in the dining room, and were at their watch post before daylight. Goose was nursing a hangover, but he sat erect and became fully alert when the front door opened. P.I. Manuel Martines walked out and picked up the morning paper.

"That bastards wearing my bathrobe!" Goose growled. "I still think I ought to go buy a gun!"

"Nope," Ben said, "you're going to Flat Land and get your new pickup and I'm going to Chalk Draw. I've got to work tomorrow, and you're most likely going to see your lawyer."

From the Ace Cafe Ben let Goose lead the way. He didn't want to take the chance of having him double back to El Paso. "Tomorrow's Monday—go see your lawyer Goose."

"I'm much obliged," Goose shook Ben's hand. "I owe you."

Ben watched the red pickup as it exited and crossed the railroad at the Badger exit. That concluded Ben's obligation and he made a beeline for Chalk Draw.

chapter XXXIV

Ben was in his customary seat at the round table when Kent arrived. He was smoking a cigarette and looking through the El Paso paper, but he folded it and put it under his leg. No out of the ordinary murders had been reported in El Paso, which eased his mind.

"Didn't you go home this weekend?"

"No," Ben said. "I got tied up and didn't make it. But I'm going home on Tuesday or Wednesday. Donna graduates from high school on Thursday the 31st and I'm going to be there. I got lucky last week and got most of my batch of the permits, so you all won't miss me while I'm off."

"You mean you're nearly through?"

"Yeah," Ben said, "but you've got to remember that I know most of the land owners west of Blessing. I've seen nearly all of them in the last thirty years. If you'll dole me out my other batch I'll work on them tomorrow, after I make one more run to Badger."

"Bill and Hal came in at the same time and were in good spirits. Ben glanced at the wall clock and saw it was past eight, so he excused himself and said he would be back as soon as he made a call. "Ya'll go ahead and order. I've already had breakfast. I should be back in fifteen minutes."

"Engineering. Ruby speaking. Can I help you?"

"This is Ben. Anybody been looking for me? I've been out of pocket since Friday."

"I called your home. Didn't your daughter tell you?"

"Yeah, she told me on Saturday morning but I wouldn't call you at home. What did you need?"

"Just a moment. I'm going to put you on hold until I get to Brad's office. He's out of town and I need privacy." He waited. "Ben, I hardly know how to say this, but I want you to hear it from me. I hope you will understand."

"Go ahead Ruby. I'm a big boy. What do you have on your mind?"

"First, I'd like to tell you that I'll always care about you. You were there when I needed someone and I'll never forget that. You will always have a special place in my heart."

"Is this a 'Dear John' call?" Ben asked.

"I guess you could call it that," Ruby stammered. "Are you O.K.?"

"I'll be fine, but you don't need to say another word. It's over—that's all there is to it. I wish you luck and the past is just that—the past. Take care of yourself and be happy. I'll be here at the Remuda until Wednesday at noon. Then I'm going to be out of pocket until next Monday. I'll check with you from time to time, or you can pass our calls along to Kent, Hal or Bill. Stay in touch."

"I'll always love you Ben. In a special way."

Ben hung up and returned to the restaurant. "I'll buy the breakfast," he said.

"You look like you got good news," Bill said. "Did you get a raise?"

"Better than that," Ben said. "My daughter graduates Thursday night and she's invited me to the ceremony!"

Kent had put a pencil to the permit completion and determined it was near the halfway mark, and both Bill and Hal had great expectations for the week ahead. Kent reported that J. J. and Bob had been in contact. They were both involved with the construction crews and working at cataloging damages to crops and pastures, which would be a great help when the lines were completed. He added that Brad was pleased with the overall situation.

Ben's first stop was at Frances Holiman's place, and as always he waited in the car for her appearance. She descended the ramp closely followed by the dog. They came to the shady spot and Frances invited Ben to his accustomed seat.

"Miss Holiman," Ben said," I'm not really here on a business call. As a matter of fact, I don't really know why I'm here—I just couldn't stay away seems like."

"I'm glad you came," she smiled. "You and Mr. Kelly did a wise thing by reacting as you did in that El Paso matter. Even your little trip across the Rio Grande is understandable."

"Did Mr. Kelley tell you of our adventures?" Ben blushed.

"I've not seen him," she admitted," but Oliver told me."

It took Ben a moment to recall just exactly who Oliver was. It was Corporal Oliver Knight of course. He may have officially perished at

Normandy, but Frances Holiman received him as a regular caller, and as crazy as it sounds, Ben believed her.

"I hope Mr. Kelly is doing well," Ben said. "I'm going to run by his place after I leave here. I've got to where I think a lot of him."

"He's got a good heart," Frances said." He is not the simple-minded person that many people think he is. And" she paused, "neither am I."

"I owe you a lot Miss Holiman. You told me what I already knew about my behavior and gave me the will power to change my ways. Someday, I may be able to help you out of a spot. When and if that time comes, all you have to do is let me know."

"You've already compensated me. You saw Mr. Kelly through a difficult time when he needed a friend. I care about him and you were my ally, so banish the thought that you are indebted to me from your mind."

They sat and talked an hour away, but the subjects were transmission line construction and the teeming animal and fowl life milling about. Miss Holiman admitted that her canine companion was not her property. As Ben had half suspected it was Moose, and belonged to Goose Kelly. He was not restrained from going home any time he chose, but he was welcome to stay with her. He was curled up at her feet as his status was discussed and appeared to have no migration urges. Goose Kelly, of course, was fully aware of Moose's location.

"I'd best be going Miss Holiman," Ben glanced at his watch. "I'll see you when the line is complete—or sooner if you call. I'll never forget what you helped me to do, and I imagine that Mr. Kelly feels the same way."

He got into his car as she and Moose followed. His arm was cradled on the rolled down glass and Frances Holiman patted it in farewell. Even though he expected the electrical impulse Ben recoiled a little. Frances smiled.

"Be careful on your journey," she said, "and be proud of your daughter. She needs a better car for her college transportation." Ben started the engine but he did not move until Frances and Moose ascended the ramp and went into the window.

Goose invited him in, and gave Ben an ashtray to hold when he was seated in his barber chair. Ben thanked him and lit up, and tilted back a notch.

"Works good don't it?"

"Like a charm," Ben said. "These are the best seats in the house. Have things been going to suit you Mr. Kelly?"

"Yeah," Goose smiled. "Wanda wants to quit her teaching and move back down here. We've got an architect working up plans for a house she can be happy with. I'm going to keep this place for my office, and resting room. She called me to congratulate me on winning my new pickup, and told me she wanted to come home."

"I'm glad everthing worked out for you Mr. Kelly. It was none of my business, but I just wanted to see that you were doing well. You don't owe me any details, but I feel good knowing that you came through the difficulties you had."

"I turned Rocket loose over in the salt cedars around the Cielo Vista River," Goose said. "He's the last turtle I'm going to train. I might go as a spectator, but I won't be entering the race again."

"You're going to give somebody else a chance to win?"

"Yeah, I won't have time to fool with training a turtle with Wanda back on the place."

"Are you going to tell me how you train your turtles?" Ben asked. "I'll keep it a secret, but I'd sure like to know. "Goose ratcheted his chair and thought the matter over.

"I'm going to tell you Ben," he decided. "You're going to laugh at how simple it is, but since I'm out of the business I'll tell you how it's done.

"That straightened coat hanger and a bottle of pepper sauce is all the equipment you need to train a turtle.

"What you do at first is tap the top of his shell a time or two with your coat hanger. Naturally he won't move until you dip the crook end into the pepper sauce and insert it to a tender spot under his shell at the back end."

"You mean to tell me that you put hot sauce up his hind end?"

"Exactly," Goose said. "It don't take that turtle long to figure out what comes next after a tap if he don't move out. It won't be long before you can forget about the pepper sauce, but that turtle don't ever forget. One tap and he's off to the races."

"You didn't have that coat hanger at the race," Ben recalled. "How'd you get him to go?"

"I dropped pea gravels on his shell," Goose reminded. "Rocket couldn't tell if I was using a coat hanger or not. They both sound the same to him."

"I'll not spread that around" Ben vowed, "but there's one other thing I need to talk to you about."

"What's that?"

"Your five thousand dollars."

"Now, Ben we've already gone over that. That ain't my money—it's yours. You won it fair and square, and the case is closed! I'll think less of you if you mention it again. Buy your daughter a graduation present."

Nothing else was left to say, and Ben decided to let the subject drop. He could not see any way of changing Goose's mind.

"Well, Mr. Kelly I'm much obliged. I've got a big job starting over east of here, but I'll be back when the construction is done on your place."

Ben got out of his chair and handed Goose the ash tray as they shook hands.

"I'm pulling for you Goose," Ben said.

"I appreciate knowing you Ben," Goose said. "But I've got the world by the tail and on a downhill pull now."

"You deserve it."

"One more thing before you hit the road," Goose smiled.

"What's that?" Ben paused at the top of the steps.

"How about a mess of butter beans?"

Ben drove away.